NATIVE GRRL

GEORGE ONSTOT

THIS IS FOR NATIVE GRRLS EVERYWHERE.

ALSO BY GEORGE ONSTOT

PUBLISHED BY

THE GOOD WORD

Call me Nedy; that's my nickname. My mum picked it out of some novel. My real name is Elizabeth Anne Ignas, the world's oldest 19-year-old and feeling older every minute. I'm starting to think that all things, especially the bad ones, were meant to happen. It's just that our egos con us into thinking that we have control over our lives. The eggheads call it determinism. Whatever it is, it's scary.

Today I visited Myles in Bayporte City Jail. We have known each other forever, literally, so it just made sense that we would meet up again early on in this life. I'm sure I will always know him. Kindred spirits are never apart for very long. I sat across from my man in the visiting room and looked at his beautiful face through six inches of Plexiglas. Into the battered black telephone I said, "Hey Myles…"

He looked up, startled. "Don't ever call me Myles," he'd once told me. "It's not personal enough." So I always call him honey or baby or sweetie, but when I called him Myles, well, he knew something was definitely *up*.

He has been in jail for two months. He sat there in his ugly orange jumpsuit and stared at me. He knew he should feel lucky to have a visitor; many of the other inmates have learned the hard way that if you want to become estranged from your friends and family, just go to jail. You'll be shocked at how your people forget you're alive.

The cops had put him in there for something he didn't do. Something had gone down, so someone needed to be punished for it. So guess who they got to serve time? We had a lawyer working to help us get through all this ugliness and bullshit.

Myles is very tough, proud and smart. He puts all of his energy into surviving incarceration because he fears he may be inside for a very long time. I freaked him out when I sat down across from him in that visiting room and said, "Hey Myles…"

So:

"Hey Myles…I'm pregnant."

He looked stunned at first, as if the pigs had Tasered him. But then his face softened and he kind of smiled, the way he does whenever someone gives him good news. He's as human as everyone else, though everyone else seems to forget that.

But then he looked really helpless and his long, narrow eyes went away into a thousand-yard stare, as if he were a shell-shocked soldier. He sat back a bit. He knew, of course, that he'd fathered my unborn child—no one else would have me—and, if he could, he would marry me right away. He surely didn't want *his* child to be born a bastard, though I didn't care about that. We'd made some casual plans before the pigs threw him in jail. Personally, I think most social conventions are idiotic; if you're in love and want to move in together and have babies, that's your business. You don't need a ring, a piece of paper and a ceremony. Your love is all that matters.

"A baby?" Myles beamed. "You're shittin me."

I rolled my eyes. "Yeah, right. I'm just trying to mess with your head."

"What do we do now?" he asked.

"We do," I said, "just what we've been doing. You sit tight while Mum and I get the lawyer to prove your innocence and get you out of here. Then we have the baby and live happily ever after."

Myles threw back his head and laughed so hard that the guard shot us a nasty look. My man looked as innocent and irresistible as a little kid. That's one of the things I love most about him. Those who don't know him very well fear him because he's big and seems mean. But he's really just an overgrown kid trying to make his way through life.

"Who else knows?"

"Just us."

He sighed. "I wonder what Parry will think." Mark Parry, Myles' father, insisted for some reason that everyone call him by his last name.

"He'll love it. I can work till it's time. My family is totally there for us. But the main thing is getting you out of here in time for the baby."

He nodded in a distracted way. I knew he wouldn't

believe he had gained his freedom until the moment he actually walked out of there and into my arms. The guard came by and pointed at the clock. We both nodded and stood up. Myles, half a head taller than I, had lost weight and his gauntness alarmed me. For a crazy moment I thought he should knock the guard flat on his ass and we could get out of there together, running just as fast as we could, holding onto one another's hand, just the way they did in the movies. But no; we did our usual thing: the Black Power salute. We're Natives—"The niggers of Canada," says Myles—so we stand there with our right arms extended and right fists clenched, like Huey Newton and Angela Davis. Then we go our separate ways.

I lived within walking distance of the jail, so I just started off towards home. Some visitors took the bus to the jail because it stopped right in front of the building. But others didn't get on or off in front of the jail because they felt embarrassed about having someone in there. I felt no shame because I knew the truth: Myles had been locked up by a cruel and racist society. I believed he would rejoin us soon and we could get past this crisis and get on with our lives.

Myles and I have been in Bayporte all our lives. We live in skid row, more properly known as the city's Lower East End, the poorest postal code in Canada. I call it the Mojave Desert of the North; if you weaken enough in the desert, the vultures and snakes will get you. In my neighborhood, the pimps and crack dealers will get to you as your spirit weakens. "Try this just once," they say as they offer you the needle or pipe. Once you're strung out, they turn you out on the street.

Of course, I have to admit that I would sell crack

and crystal meth all day and night if I could make enough money to get Myles the best defense lawyer in town. My man has endured it all so far; a lesser man would have hanged himself by now. But I know that under his tough-as-iron exterior, he's as scared as I am, and we both know that our predicament may simply get worse. We can't just keep coping and being tough indefinitely.

Adversity can make people stronger, but it can also make us more cynical. I have seen the faces of the people on the bus going past the jail. People, seeing me emerge from the jail, have sneered at me and probably feared sitting next to me on the bench or bus because of some dreadful disease I've gotten from my jailbird. I'm tempted to say to them, "I've just been visiting my boyfriend, Myles, in jail. He's innocent and I'm pregnant. We need money for legal fees. Can you help us out?"

I don't think so. This is our problem, not theirs. I have a family and a full-time job; I get enough to eat—even for two. But I have made up my mind about something: When this ordeal ends, Myles and I will run away from home. Until Myles got busted, I thought Bayporte a fine place to live, even if we were stuck in skid row. But now I believe that Bayporte is the scummiest, sleaziest, most wretched place imaginable. I cannot forgive the way they have treated Myles, and that colors my perception of this entire city.

I remember all those weekends when Dad used to take us to Pioneer Park for the day. We would walk every trail and stuff our faces with fish and chips, pop and candy. Then we would walk all the way back home. I loved those outings because I got to spend so much time with Dad, and Rose was afraid to pick on me in front of him. But now I see this city as a nasty place; every day, I have to step over needles, syringes and condoms on my way to work.

...

Myles and I went to an elementary school just a few blocks away. Our classmates, naturally, were "high risk" Natives whose families, for some generations, had some difficulty in keeping their "social fabric intact," as the textbooks say.

Myles' family lived just a block from us. His father had run Parry's Smoke Shop, one of the Lower East End's most popular businesses, for as long as I could remember. Parry sold every brand of cigarettes imaginable, plus snacks, pop, and gross-out beaver magazines. He hated selling crack pipes but did so because so many people kept asking for them. Myles told me that his father kept a loaded .38 revolver under his cash register because he accepted cash but not credit cards. He needn't have feared a robbery because the police station was half a block away. many of us felt proud to have one of our own running his own successful business, even a hole-in-the-wall smoke shop. Chinatown, two minutes away, had had many more small-business proprietors over the years. Dad told me that back in the 1970s, Chinatown fairly bustled with shops, restaurants and nightclubs. Maybe then, but not now. So many Chinese fled to the suburbs and took their money with them. The ones who remained complained that bums from skid row had wandered over to panhandle Chinatown's tourists. Our lot would get worse before it got better, Dad said.

Myles and I got to know each other mainly because of a fistfight. I was 10 and he was 12, and we weren't yet of much interest to each other. Wild Mary, Myles, his best friend Pete and I had gone over to Munro Park, not far from the harbor. Thanks to so much rain, Munro Park stayed green throughout the year and had a wonderful view of the water and mountains to the north. The park also had benches and monkey bars and could be a fun place to spend the day if you were too poor to go anywhere else. The park had sat desolate for some years before tourism executives or people with similar power got after the city's parks and recreation board to rehabilitate the aging, rotting park.

The handful of white kids already there beat it when they saw us coming, four rowdy Natives whooping it up, high-fiving each other and getting ready to do some serious hanging out. Myles had heard rumors about homosexual orgies happening in the men's washroom, so he and Pete went in to check things out. They came out after two minutes, shaking their heads.

"See anything good?" asked Wild Mary, my best friend. She got me into plenty of trouble. A big, brash girl, she said or did whatever she thought might get her the most attention. At school they'd held her back twice, and so we were classmates despite our age difference. Wild Mary cared very little about grades and passing; she dared the teachers to hold her back till she was 30.

I had given her that nickname, and she always smiled at the sound of it, unaware that I hadn't meant it altogether as a compliment. She came across to me as one of those kids who had traded in tomorrow for today and refused to let anyone ruin her good time. Wild Mary just did her thing, and fuck you too if you didn't like it. she believed that, as a minor, she could act out with impunity. She felt sure that she would outlive us all and dance on our graves. I figured her luck would run out; she would have a future of single motherhood, jail time, halfway houses and minimum-wage work, if any. But back then, I couldn't resist her and we had the greatest fun together. Even so, I knew our essential differences would end our friendship soon.

So the four of spent the day together at Munro Park, the boys and girls checking out each other while pretending to do just the opposite. I remember the day as being brisk and breezy, with clayey clouds blowing across the sky. Seagulls cawed overhead and I feared they would drop birdshit on us. Wild Mary and I sat on the swings, whispering to each other as Myles and Pete clowned around on the monkey bars. Mary muttered some really nasty things about Myles, the way you do when you really like someone and are completely uncomfortable with your feelings. She said he must be the ugliest goof alive, so tall and skinny, and his narrow eyes made him look dishonest. Then she tugged at her ponytail and earring, which were very much like his, and mouthed, *He looks like a faggot.*

I thought his ponytail and earring looked exotic. Mary had plenty more to say about him. She claimed that he looked like those Injuns she had seen in those John Wayne movies late at night. Mary often had lots of trouble finding her own ass with both hands, but she did know about movies; she'd stay up all night watching TV, then stay home from school or fall asleep in class. She predicted to me that Myles would have the same life I had secretly predicted for her. His friends, she said, were the meanest, toughest, most ruthless badasses in the neighborhood. She insisted that she had seen him with his pals in the basement of a condemned building with some girl. They "did it" with her standing up—I didn't ask her to define "did it" for fear she would laugh at me at tell everyone about my ignorance—and then, when the girl demanded money, Myles pulled out a switchblade.

I told Wild Mary she was a freaking liar. Myles didn't own a switchblade and had a kind smile, a soft voice. I watched him cavort on the monkey bars—a knife-wielding tough guy who screwed chicks in abandoned basements didn't diddle around on jungle gyms. I also thought that if he looked like a late-show Injun, I should stay up and watch those shows.

At that age, I understood very little about

infatuation, so I really thought that Mary hated Myles and Pete because of all her bickering with them. So, that afternoon, Mary started in on them and soon they started shoving each other. I tried to pry them apart. Myles lost his balance, went sprawling into the monkey cars and banged his head. He blacked out for several moments and we saw blood trickling from his ear.

Wild Mary freaked out, screaming that I had killed Myles or at least given him severe brain damage, and that if by some miracle he survived, he'd be too retarded to have any friends. But within minutes he seemed his old self again and wandered off with Pete. Mary stormed off a little later, and I sat there in Munro Park all alone, hating myself for what an awful thing I had done and what a horrible person I surely was.

Over the following days, Wild Mary told me that Myles was barely alive in the ICU at Bayporte General Hospital, and my parents should expect the cops to come by any day now to take me away in handcuffs and charge me with attempted murder. But when I walked past Parry's Smoke Shop and Mr. Parry smiled and waved for me to come in, I watched him ring up a purchase of Player's Lights and *Hustler* magazine. He seemed to be taking his son's tragedy quite well.

"Hi, Nedy. How's it goin? Nice day out there, hey?"

I smiled and glanced around the store. Guys at the magazine rack shot me a curious look. Nice girls weren't supposed to be in places like *that*.

"Hi, Mr. Parry. Everything's OK." I wanted to scream, *Aren't you mad at me for trying to kill your only son? Do you know if the cops have any leads?*

"I think your boyfriend will be back soon," he said.

I frowned. "What are you talking about?"

He chuckled. "Myles. He's been away for a little while. Haven't you missed him?"

I didn't know what to say or do. Surely Myles was on an IV, with a guard at the door to make sure that nobody came by to finish the job…?

"His mum," said Parry, "sent him out to the country because he and his hoodlum friends were just getting a bit too bossy for their own good." He sighed. "As if he can't get into any trouble out there in the country. I wish he would take some of that energy he puts into showing off for his friends and use it to improve himself." He smiled sadly, and I saw just how much father and son looked alike.

"Tell him I said hi, Mr. Parry," I said as I hurried out the door and ran all the way to Munro Park, where Wild Mary frittered away so much of her time.

"A lot *you* know, Mary Burke," I said as I confronted her at the monkey bars. "Parry just told me that Myles is in the country, not the hospital." Unable to think of anything else to say, I turned around and walked home.

. . .

When Myles returned home from the country, he seemed normal and functional. We walked down to the harbor together and shared an ice-cold pop. We sat on a bench and stifled belches as we gazed at the mighty, beautiful Tyson River. The sky shone the deepest cobalt blue and a brisk wind messed up our hair. Myles sat by my side and I felt better than alive.

'I'm glad you're not still mad at me,' he said.

'I'm glad you're not in the ICU,' I said.

I guess you could say that our friendship began that day. An odd thing, maybe, a boy and girl being friends at that age. Inappropriate, even. But I think we needed each other. I regarded my sibling with ambivalence and he had nothing but loathing for his. So we filled a void for each other, voids that quite needed filling.

I seldom saw Wild Mary after that. She probably thought I hated her, so she terminated our friendship; or maybe *I* cut *her* loose. Who knows *how* kids' friendships end? (Or adults', for that natter.) Myles and Pete had quite a row over my age and Myles' relationship with me—Pete called him a pedophile—and when I offered to get my dad to beat the shit out of Pete for saying such a thing, Myles told me that I was nothing but a girl and didn't know anything about it.

Myles' mum made him attend church with her every week. His two sisters, those darling little angels hardly needing salvation, got to stay at home, sleep late and watch TV on Sunday. A devout Christian, Mrs. Parry yearned to rise above the squalor of skid row—or at least impress everyone at church with her pretty, righteous self. She seemed convinced that we were in skid row because we had somehow offended God; *I* thought the white man had stuck us in this smelly, decrepit little corner of the city and we let him get away with it. Mrs. Parry said we needed to get into God's good graces by going to church and obeying the preacher. So she went there religiously, so to speak, and made sure she had wayward little Myles by her side. If Mr. Parry refused to join them, well, too bad for him and his soul.

Myles and I felt that he belonged to a one-parent family. He was *his* son or *hers* but never *theirs*. Maybe that explained some of his restlessness and acting out. once you took the time and trouble to get to know him, you discovered his sensitive and caring side. Parry, instead of trying to remake his son. Simply accepted him. Anya and Talia, Myles' two sisters, tried to emulates their mother's dainty-lady ways and occasionally succeeded. Parry, to pacify his missus, made Myles go to church with her, thinking it wouldn't do any harm and might actually do the boy a bit of good. Mrs. Parry wanted to show her church friends what an upstanding and outstanding little man she had. She would never have called herself a feminist, but *I* would, and not as a compliment. She had crippled Myles with her feminism; he lived in fear, whether or not he realized it, of being made a eunuch by the women in his life. He probably considered himself doomed to eternal childhood and wondered at the same time if another woman—me— was the answer he needed.

Myles did his thing on the streets, and Parry did *his* in the store. Myles hung out with his buddies and got the gratification and satisfaction he needed from their admiration and approval of him. Parry sought female succor in his wife and daughters; finding none, and eager to escape their oppression, he ran away from home each day for ten hours or more to his smoke shop. He *schmoozed* with his customers and sold them the cancer sticks, junk food and stroke books they craved. 'I want to run this place for the rest of my life. It sure beats working,' he told his customers. Whenever Myles came home with a black eye or split lip, Parry cleaned him up and didn't ask about the fight. Myles had simply done what he needed to do.

Parry, knowing that I loved Myles unconditionally, loved me like a father, while his son loved me like a lover. I used wonder about Mr. and Mrs. Parry and once asked Myles, "Do your parents still...do it?"

He laughed. "Yeah, but they have their own way. After Mum gets home from church, that's about the time he wants her the most. After she'd been shouting out praises to God and getting all rapturous and sweaty, and she would go into the bedroom to change out of her Sunday best but she would lay on the bed, sayin she was too tired to take off her clothes, so he'd help her with that. She'd lay there in a heap on the bed, saying, 'Oh, Parry, God don't want us doing that after I've just finished worshiping Him.' And he'd be getting all horny, saying, 'If you don't get out of those wet clothes, you'll catch pneumonia and meet Him sooner than you think.' That's their game, right? She wants to get it on as much as he does but she won't admit it because she thinks sex is a sin. They need this game to keep their thing going.

"So he's getting naked and pulling off her sweaty things, and all the while she's saying, 'Oh, Parry, you need to go to church and find God.' And he says, 'I *am* God and I am coming to thee. Where do you want your blessing, child? You are my temple; where shall I enter you? I will give you a second coming, and a third.' So on it goes, with moaning and groaning. Then, the next moaning, she goes back to being Ms. Pious and he goes back to the smoke shop."

Myles paused, looking sad. "He's not a happy man. He probably would have left us a long time ago, except his conscience wouldn't let him. Also, he loves running that store. That's what keeps him going."

I loved Parry for being there. I don't imagine the Parrys laughed when they made love the way Myles and I did. Laughter, love and all of our best emotions come from the same place within each of us. It's such a shame that we don't visit that place often enough.

. . .

"Nedy," Myles said, "I want you to go to church with us." I said yes; I wanted it to be our "coming out," although most of the people at the First Nations Church already knew that he and I were "special friends." Myles, if anything, had become agnostic from so much exposure to Christianity, and I suppose

I found it all too baffling to take it seriously, so that made *me* agnostic, too.

Myles looked miserable in the blue polywool suit his mum had picked out for him. I didn't much like the dress my mum had stuffed *me* into, either. But there we were, two poor Native kids all prettied up to go to church and say, "How's it goin, eh?" to the deity who had shorted us on goodies. You might say that Myles and I were on our very first date, although we didn't see it that way. I wanted a date where his mum didn't chaperone us. I wanted my man to pick me up, take me out for dinner, dancing and a nice long makeout session in his car. I knew, during our church "date" that our dates could only get better.

Myles and Mrs. Parry waited for me outside their apartment building. I walked up to them, waving and smiling, on a springtime Sunday morning, neither warm nor cool, not sunny and not fun. Mrs. Parry surely thought it odd that her son would have a friend—OK, a girlfriend—at such a young age, and that his girlfriend would be an ungainly little thing like me. Myles, of course, hadn't slipped the ring onto my finger just yet, and maybe his mother already saw that her son would, in a few years, become a tall, handsome, charismatic young stud who could pick and choose when it came to women. She really didn't love him, I don't think. At least not the way Parry did. But she did feel an obligation to pretend that she did love him, if loving meant browbeating and criticizing him and dragging him off to church.

Mrs. Parry disliked me, too, although I came across as far too meek and mild for het to regard me with much more than everyday contempt. Myles came to my home but I rarely went to his; and when I did, I felt deeply unwelcome and uncomfortable. Mrs. Parry and her daughters disliked me because they considered me less than he deserved, or they felt *I* considered *him* less than *I* deserved...or maybe they just got pissed off because I liked him so much. I had never viewed myself as being the remotest threat to anyone, with my broad nose, unruly hair and curveless body. When I had reached adolescence and got all the tits and ass I would ever get, even Myles didn't pretend that he found me physically attractive. He said it didn't matter; pretty girls were nothing but a hassle.

Pretty girls were nothing but a hassle. Mrs. Parry, in her youth, had been very pretty. Were daughters were, too, but less so, and all three shared that museum quality of being very cold and never to be touched. They all had fine Caucasoid features and red-tan complexions. Myles, in all ways his father's son, had sharp, ruggedly handsome features and none of his mother's conventional prettiness.

"I'm glad you're joining us this morning, Nedy," Mrs. Parry said, smiling or grimacing (sometimes I couldn't tell with her). "You certainly look clean and pretty."

"Thank you, ma'am," I said.

On Sunday morning, the people of skid row, hung over and strung out, slept late and behaved themselves. The night before, as always, fights had started in pubs and ended in the streets. Crackheads tweaked like white-faced mimes and prostitutes did their thing on each corner. Through these streets we now walked to praise God and seek salvation.

"Maybe," said Mrs. Parry as we walked down the

mostly empty streets, "your mum and dad could join us sometime. Which church do you usually attend?"

"We don't," I said, telling her something she already knew.

Mrs. Parry tsked. "That's too bad. So this is a special occasion for you, hey?"

"Yes, ma'am." I looked at Myles and we smiled at each other. All of our get-togethers were special occasions. We walked on, not saying much. Myles used to have to go to Sunday School at nine in the morning, and often needed some help in getting himself together and arriving there on time. The walk from his home to Sunday school had some of the best bad things in downtown Bayporte; unescorted, he usually got hung up with one distraction or another and didn't get to Sunday school at all. His mother, a woman of remarkable laziness, would hear the alarm, yell at her son to get up, then she'd roll over and go back to sleep. 'My mum didn't worry,' he told me. 'She said that Jesus would look out for me.'

So: we went to the "old bank," as we called the First Nations Church, which still looked very much like the Bank of Toronto building. The floor's faded, scuffed tiles had the ubiquitous BT logo not deemed worth the trouble and expense of replacing, and I could see where the tellers' wickets had been. The bank moved out after people kept robbing it, and the building stayed vacant until the church took over. I swore I could smell the traces of paper money in the dusty air. The money that had come in, gone out and been obsessed over—*that* god, evident and tangible, had commanded a zeal as intense as anything these Bible-thumpers felt for *their* deity in the sky. Sitting on that wooden bench, with my bum getting sore and my eyes starting to water from Mrs. Parry's perfume, I chuckled to myself at the notion that the Bank of Toronto, every bit as much as the First Nations Church, was a place of worship.

Rows of benches filled the church, and the pulpit seemed a mile away. But to Mrs. Parry, that mattered very little; she loved having this big old place as *her* church, just as the others valued it so much as *theirs*, and Mrs. Perry claimed that her church had greater seating capacity and better acoustics than the one at West Shore, the part of town where all the rich people lived. She carried on like a celebrity in there, smiling and waving, as if her salvation were a done deal. She probably thought I had to go through her to get to Him, as if she were His representative on earth. We sat in the mercy seat, in the front row. While

Myles and I sat and waited, Mrs. Parry knelt and prayed, with a very grave countenance. Then she turned around, nodded at those behind us, and sat. I looked at Myles, and he just shrugged, so I shrugged back. I wished he and I were at the harbor, sharing a pop and watching the whitecaps. Even in my Sunday best, I looked like a morose Native kid in a discount-store dress, and poor Myles looked like Old Glory in his blue suit, white shirt and red tie.

Myself, I could never see the sense in praying. I just felt like I was talking to myself when I put my hands together and looked up or closed my eyes and asked the busy Creator to intercede in my trivial matters. Did Mrs. Parry think she could pray her way out of the Lower East End? Was that her game? She seemed to pray for things to happen or not to happen; I thought she would be better off praying for the strength to cope with whatever bad stuff *did* happen. I smiled as I watched Mrs. Parry silently ask God to take care of her business. Who did she think He was? Christianity had made Him into a wise, tough old white man who'd sent His son to die on a cross. So, whenever Mrs. Parry asked for deliverance from skid row and He said no, she just asked Him some more.

At the First Nations Church, they did things a bit differently. This was a sort of Gospel/Harlem/Bible Belt place. They expressed themselves as the spirit moved them, literally, and they "testified," meaning that some of the parishioners stood up and spoke to us all about how God have saved them from drugs, insanity, violence and whatever else had tried to do them in. Darnell, a big Native boy I had seen staggering around countless times, told us, with a passion and loudness that made me blush, about how God had "cured" him of his "incurable" addiction to crack cocaine. After each sentence he spoke, everyone—except Myles and me—cried out, "Praise Jesus!" Darnell, sweating like a sow after spilling his guts, sat down. A few years later, and after a handful of relapses, he died.

Then people started singing and singing some more. Myles looked at me and I mouthed, *Are we having fun yet?* We both giggled and held hands. I wondered if those people singing and carrying on were expressing love, or what. I knew what love was. Love sat right next to me, holding my hand, sweating into his blue suit. He and I were closer to God than those church people could have ever imagined.

. . .

I've thought back sometimes to that Sunday morning, to Mrs. Parry and her stylish clothes and ballsy singing, and all that screaming and shouting that happened all around us as Myles and I clung to each other like a couple of terrified kids on a roller coaster. All that craziness—and I *did* perceive it as just that—happened around us while excluding us, but that didn't matter.

Myles insisted that I decline on his mum's future church invitations unless I actually wanted to go, which I certainly did not. But with the passing of time, our morning together at the First Nations Church became something we should, and did, laugh about. But I had trouble when, for the sake of levity, I reminded him of it in that jailhouse visiting room. With the clock ticking and the guard waiting to come by and terminate our conversation, we felt we had more pressing things to say to one another.

After telling him about our baby, I walked home, wondering about how to tell Mum, Dad and Rose. Turning up the street, I felt so reluctant to go home that I nearly headed to the nearest downtown shopping mall for a chocolate milkshake. But I had no money for such treats, especially expensive ones, and expensive treats were the only kinds downtown Bayporte sold.

Mum, always the dominant person in my life and Rose's, is getting middle-aged and gray now, and increasingly set in her ways, which I consider a good thing. Her name is June, and she, is one of my very favorite people in the world, even when she is stubborn and strict. Born and raised in the Prairies, she says little about her childhood in Manitoba, besides calling it flat and boring. Passably pretty in her youth, she could sing well enough to join a five-piece rock band. She wanted the musical career that, years later, Alanis Morissette got; that didn't happen, but she did tour her way out of Manitoba. In their van, they traveled all over Canada, getting one-night stands everywhere because they sounded adequate and worked cheaply. From that experience, she learned that she lacked the talent and galloping ambition to become a music-business success. 'The drummer and I had an affair,' she recalled. 'It didn't work out, and we all called it quits in Toronto. I decided to head out to Bayporte, because I liked it the best of all the cities I had been to.'

So Mum spent a few days and nights on the westbound bus, swapping truths and lies with whoever sat next to her. They rolled their eyes when they asked her destination and she told them she was riding the Dirty Dog all the way to Bayporte.

Mum's schedule terminated in Calgary, and her connection to Bayporte would depart in two hours, so she sat in the big, overlit lobby, wondering how long her pocketful of petty cash would last. She resisted the urge to plunk some change into the vending machines and pig out on candy.

My dad, Mark Ignas, the station's security guard, had almost finished his shift. Years earlier, his high school guidance counselor had pushed him towards police work because of his imposing size and because the police department could always use another Native officer. But Dad didn't want to arrest people and get shot or spat at; he didn't want to hang out at a Greyhound station for forty hours a week, either, telling runaways, throwaways and sexual predators to buy a ticket or go away.

At his age, Dad still hadn't figured out who he wanted to be when he grew up.

So naturally Dad saw Mum, a really cute Native girl sitting there with no boyfriend or husband in sight, and he thought: *She's the one.* Mum tried to look hip, savvy and streetwise, but Dad just saw a scared, lonely little girl.

He walked up to her and asked, 'Are you going to Bayporte?'

'Yes,' she said, wondering why he had asked and she answered.

'Then so am I.' He sat down next to her.

'Looks like you work here.' Mum smirked at the loafing guard. 'That's a handsome uniform.'

'I just quit,' he told her. 'As soon as you walked in,

I got a better idea about what to do with my life.'

'I'm sure Greyhound needs you a lot more than I do.'

'Say, do you know Bayporte well?'

'Yes,' she lied.

'Do you know'—he mentioned an address he had never heard of—'it's in downtown Batporte. My dad lives there.'

'I think that's in Chinatown,' she said.

'Well,' he said, 'my dad is a Chinaman.'

Mum wanted to get the security guard to shoo away this weirdo, but of course the weirdo *was* the guard.

'I'll be right back,' Dad said. He ran back to his

aging SRO hotel room and stuffed his few possessions into his only suitcase. He had always believed that opportunity would knock one day, and when it did, he wanted to be ready. A bunch of belongings would only slow him down. After checking out, he ran back to the Greyhound station with his guard uniform in one hand and his suitcase in the other. He had changed into his best shirt and slacks. He left his uniform in the guard's office without a note, then bought a one-way ticket to Bayporte from the puzzled clerk and sat down next to Mum. 'That was the dumbest, rashest thing I have ever done,' he told me. 'But I don't regret it for a moment.'

They boarded the bus and sat together. Mum, stupefied by exhaustion, fell asleep right away and slept for most of the trip. Dad sort of arranged her across his lap, wondering how long his money would last and if this pretty young thing would still want to have anything to do with him once the bus pulled into the TransCanada Railway Station and he nudged her awake with the words, 'We're here.'

Well, obviously, things worked out for them. Mum stayed at a place called the Bayporte Women's Residence and Dad holed up in a flop called the Winton Hotel. They've been together ever since and are still trying to escape skid row.

...

I felt tired and sweaty when I got home. We live on the third floor of a moderately affordable building that doesn't yet reek of feces and urine. Our neighborhood has places to live that are infinitely worse. Myles dreams of sharing an artist's loft with me near Pioneer Park. He wants to make a living by carving amazing things out of local wood. He believes that with enough determination and encouragement, he can do it.

Mum probably already knows about my baby, and if she doesn't, she won't be surprised; she's too worldly for that. Dad will fret over the practical side of things: I'm unmarried; my man is in jail and his lawyer isn't working for free; there will be another mouth to feed in eight months.

I sat in the kitchen as Mum came in, her heels clicking on the linoleum floor. She smiled at me. "How's our boy today?"

"He's OK." I sighed. "He's not sure if he's the best lawyer in town, but he says he got who he got."

Mum harrumphed. "Lawyers. Damn them all."

Then she started supper, and soon things on the stove started steaming up and smelling good. She stood there, doing her thing, and I sat near her, unable to figure out how to tell her the biggest news of my young life. I closed my eyes and just spat it out.

"Mum, I'm pregnant."

I opened my eyes and saw her staring at me.

"Was that so hard," she asked me, "that you had to close your eyes?"

Just then, Rose came in. "Watch the stove," Mum said to her, then took me into her bedroom. We sat on the bed and I started to cry.

"Why the tears? Did you tell Myles today?"

I nodded, snuffling.

"Well, *that* must have brightened his day a bit,

hey?"

"I guess." I wiped my nose on the sleeve of my blouse. "It freaked him out."

Mum chuckled. She smoothed her skirt, as if the words she sought lay somewhere in its folds. "Nedy," she said, "I want you to stop those tears. You have nothing to be ashamed of. Even though you're unmarried, this pregnancy says nothing bad about your character. Of course, Parry's wife will have something to say about it when she finds out. We are a proud family and a proud people. This is our home. The white people got here by accident and stole it from us. Now they have *your* man locked up because of their foolish justice system. You and Myles should be together and happy right now. He has two reasons to live: you and the baby. You must look after yourself and stay strong for him. We *will* get him out, but while he's still in there, you've got to be strong for him and keep the faith, because if you don't, he will die."

I swallowed hard and nodded. "I hear you, Mum."

She smiled. "After supper, you and I will tell Dad and Rose that great news."

I nodded. "I'm OK with that."

"Then that's what we'll do." She patted my thigh and said, "Now, if you'll excuse me, I need to get back to the kitchen before your sister destroys supper and burns down the apartment building."

She got up, and as she reached the doorway, I said, "Mum?"

"Yes, Nedy?"

"Thanks."

"For what?"

I shrugged. "Thanks for being you."

Mum laughed. "Well, I'm just being the only person I *can* be. But it's nice to be appreciated."

Then she left the room. I lay on the bed with my eyes closed and listened as the front door opened and closed. Dad.

"Is Nedy home?" he asked Mum.

"Yes."

"Did she see Myles today?"

"Of course she did," said Mum. "He's surviving."

"What's the lawyer doing to get him out?"

"All he can, I assume."

Dad grunted. I heard his heavy tread as he headed

into the kitchen for his pre-dinner can of beer. "I have a feeling"—I heard the anger rumbling in his deep voice—"that Beadle isn't done picking our pockets. How much more money do you think—"

"Mark, how would *I* know?"

"Well, he's probably going to ask the Parrys and us for money we don't have. Bastards."

I could picture Mum at the stove, stirring this and tasting that, wondering about what was and could be. Cursing herself for not having eyes in the back of her head and the ability to see around corners.

"So," she asked, "how was work?"

"Fine." Dad worked as a decently paid guard at an indecently smelly reduction plant. "Fine" meant that the myriad seagulls, attracted to the reek of the rendering process, didn't shit on him. Other days, he had less luck and Mum had to launder his uniform.

In our living room we had a gift from Myles: a carved figure of a man who, for some reason, reminded me of Dad. Myles had gotten hold of a footlong piece of redwood and shaved it down into a very lifelike, detailed piece of art. The man clearly was naked. I found it odd that my boyfriend would give a wooden naked man to my mum. (I told Myles how relieved I felt that he didn't give his little naked man a woody.)

Myles attended a vocational high school where they mainly taught him and the others to make desks, chests of drawers and other such pieces of furniture for which virtually no market existed. 'We made that stuff just so we'd stay busy,' Myles told me. 'That handmade furniture? Shit, Nedy, we couldn't give it away. Everybody who wants furniture can get the best stuff at a department store.'

Myles believed that the people who ran the school treated their students like a bunch of mental defectives who needed to use their brawn because they had no brains. Those kids weren't dumb, but their teachers treated them like dummies, so most of them thought they were stupid. Perhaps the school just wanted them to be good boys and girls who would grow up to be good men and women who knew how to do *something*, but often they grew up to become angry, frustrated adults who considered themselves idiots.

If you are a Lower East End kid, the social order obliges you to submit to an existence in an impoverished neighborhood where low-paying, go-nowhere jobs await you in food service or contract security. The economic machine, in order to keep humming and make rich people richer, needs you to work practically for free. So, your destiny is to be a poor person working hard to support a capitalist system that values you very little while demanding that you value *it* a great deal.

Ignorance, of course, is not bliss; rather, it is unconsciousness and slavery. Only sentience and intelligence can make us free us and allow us to become the shapers of our own destinies. We start out, like Myles' wood carvings, as raw materials being made into different things by other people. At some point, if we have the energy and will to do so, we can remake ourselves using the materials the world has given us whether you are an astronaut, a millionaire, an athlete or a Native kid in Bayporte's Lower East End, you are whatever society has made of you. If and when you remake yourself, you often end up a different person from the one you expected to become. This remaking process is a form of freedom, but it is not a cheerful thing.

You may have often asked yourself. "Who am I?" You are your being, and too often, much of your being is your job, and your workplace—the fast food restaurant, the rendering plant—becomes an extension of your being and grinds you down. Your personal growth—your desire or will to remake yourself—stalls or stops altogether because you lose the physical, emotional and spiritual stamina necessary for your quest for self-improvement. Other people and social institutions, of course, have forced this upon you, so it's hell on earth.

Is there hope for a better life? Naturally there is. But it takes a great deal of energy and courage to change one's life. One's existence has to be intolerable; and when it's tolerable, it's actually worse, because complacency will set in and stunt our growth. Anomie will be the result. We consume objects that others make, and they consume what we make. But we never meet each other except through these objects. We serve these objects more than they serve us. They get in our way, just as a book gets in the way of valid, honest communication between its writer and reader.

. . .

After a couple of years, Myles dropped out of the vocational school, but before leaving he and some friends looted the school's workshop. He told me they had way too much fine local wood—plus all those new tools!—so he and his boys went in one evening, jimmied open the door, helped themselves to all they could carry, loaded it into their car and stored it in his friend's house. The school probably didn't even investigate the theft; it simply replenished what had been taken. To the school, it may have been mere wood and metal, but to Myles, it represented a whole new life; he could now make beautiful art instead of household objects no one wanted to buy. The school certainly thought him a bad boy who had no desire to make, or be, good. But to me, being *good* does not mean being brainless and obedient. Goodness without ability is useless; all the virtue in the world will not save you if you lack intelligence.

Being an artist saved Myles from the spiritual death that threatened all of us. The Establishment told all Natives that we were worthless, and so many of us believed that. To deaden the pain that came with such condemnation, so many Native kids resorted to booze, heroin and crack. Full of rage, they acted out, stealing, mugging and beating up on people. But I didn't have to worry about Myles. He had his art and completely lost himself in it. He got a small studio and just worked, worked, worked. If I didn't see him, I certainly knew where to find him.

Myles went to our place more than to his own. His mum didn't like him; she scowled at him or ignored him, and so did his sisters because they didn't know any better. The girls were increasingly filled with panic because throughout their childhood their mum had promised them handsome husbands providing unconditional, eternal love and a way out of the Lower East End. But where were those men, now that the girls were well into their twenties? The problem was obvious to all but them—the men they knew failed to meet their standards. Both of them had graduated from Bayporte College, where the few Native men—the sisters wanted Natives—already had women or just weren't interested in the Parry girls. Mrs. Parry blamed it on Myles; if Charles Manson had broken out of prison, she would have blamed her son for *that*, too. And Myles couldn't defend himself; he didn't know how because these women simply overwhelmed him. His father, motivated by the same fear and confusion, started working seven days a week, to have an excuse to be away from home. By then many of legitimate businesses in our area had folded after decades of survival and all other local businesses were vulnerable until our economy rebounded, which it inevitably would but nobody knew when or how long the lean times would continue. Parry knew his smoke shop would always struggle because most of his income came from cigarettes and all those years of anti-smoking education and those no-smoking bylaws had reduced his sales. Plus, this *was* downtown Bayporte, albeit the undesirable part, and real-estate values would surely rise. You didn't need a master's degree urban planning to know how gentrification, which was not necessarily a good thing, would affect us here in the Lower East End.

Myles would go off on his own and Parry would come by our place, ostensibly looking for him, and end up inviting my dad out for a beer. That was OK; my dad always said Parry didn't need an invitation to come by; he was welcome whenever he felt like coming to our place. The bars were tolerable places once they outlawed smoking or confined it to restricted areas. The best thing about Myles—his passion for life and his pride—was, oddly, his most vulnerable quality. Myles Parry refused to become anyone's fool, and a Native in the East End of Bayporte who was nobody's fool was a suspicious and dangerous character fit to be locked up. At least that's what white people seemed to believe, and, I guessed, that was at the heart of Myles' troubles.

. . .

Long, tall Rose, cranky and tired, has just gotten in. She's speaking to Dad.

She works as the assistant director of the Lower East End Community Center, which is about five minutes from our home, if she walks slowly.

Mum thought that Rose, when small, should have been named Vanity. The child somehow intuitively understood that she simply had more beauty than all the other little girls and insisted on being meticulously groomed. She could have stood in front of the mirror all day long. She had a few years on me and pretended that I didn't exist. I hated her at first, but then retaliated by pretending that *she* didn't exist. She hated me back, and our screaming matches were daily occurrences.

Mum actually laughed at Rose's narcissism and our conflicts. She simply assumed that Rosie—I called her that back then just to piss her off, plus I thought that Rosie sounded less stuffy than Rose and I wanted my sister to be less stuffy—*was* temperamental in the way that a lot of gorgeous females were. Mum advised me to have a sense of humor when dealing with her. Mum became concerned that Rose, a beautiful, attention-hungry female nearing puberty, might bugger off to Los Angeles when she turned eighteen, despite having no green card, and take her chances in show business. Mum herself had done something like that, with much frustration and only moderate success, and probably had nightmares of her vain, gullible daughter being exploited and manipulated by Hollywood opportunists.

But then Rose changed. Sometime during her teens, she grew tall and voluptuous but, ironically, also started taking herself more seriously. She discovered books and decided that they held all the answers she needed. She brought home armloads of dog-eared philosophy paperbacks from the public library: Socrates, Kant, Heidegger, Sartre, Fuller. She dressed simply and tied up her hair so it wouldn't be in the way. She swore off newspapers, TV, radio and movies. Once, while Dad was reading the newspaper, she flicked at it with her fingernail and said, "Propaganda, lies and bullshit." But she wasn't mean;

in fact, if anything, she became diplomatic with me and everyone else. She said little, just read thick books and kept to herself, looking distracted, as if those dead philosophers had given her an awful lot to think about. Her face grew thinner and darker, and her deep brown eyes widened as if in response to all she had become able to see.

She didn't even apply to Northup University—"All universities are obsolete"—and instead started working for the Lower East End Residents' Association; through them, Rose got her job at the community center. It's stressful, challenging work, and I guess that's why she likes it. The center, open every day of the year, is filled mainly with Natives, drug addicts and old folks from Chinatown. The place stays open because of aggressive, relentless fundraising and an army of volunteers. Rose earns every dime of her salary, and helps with our bills.

"Where's the whore?" she asked, meaning me. I worked at Dunsmuir, the tony department store. Wanting to be perceived as an open-minded, equal-opportunity employer, they installed me, a skinny little aboriginal girl, in the perfume section so that rich white and Chinese yuppies could smell my scented wrist all day. Once, when I came home reeking of an insanely expensive fragrance, Rose walked up to me, sniffed loudly, pinched her nose and said, "Who farted?"

"Nedy is in my bedroom," Mum said. "She's lying down. She saw Myles today."

"How's he coping?" Rose asked.

"As best he can."

"Well, I'm getting hungry. Want me to start dinner?" Rose always seemed to want to show Mum she could cook, which she couldn't.

"No," Mum said. "I'll get to it in a moment."

"Has she seen Beadle yet?"

Larry Beadle, our downtown lawyer, said that our boy's freedom meant as much to him as it did to us. I doubted that. Still, Rose, who had met him when he did a bit of pro bono work to help keep the community center alive, said we were lucky to have him on our side.

"Nedy is going to see him Monday afternoon," Mum said.

"Alone?" Rose asked.

"No, with me."

"Well, that's probably for the best," Rose said. Then, "Dad, if you drink any more of that beer, we're going to have to send you to Weight Watchers or Alcoholics Anonymous. Or both."

"Don't worry about it, disrespectful one," Dad said. After a pause he added, "You know, Nedy thinks Beadle might start asking for more money."

"Well, he won't get any," Rose said. "We've already paid him a retainer, which was more than we could afford. It's supposed to keep Beadle going till he brings Myles to trial."

"Well, Beadle says the case so far doesn't look good for Myles," Mum said.

"Beadle is a lawyer," Rose said. "He's *supposed* to find ways of getting his client off. Maybe we should call those guys who represented O.J. Simpson."

Mum and Dad laughed.

"Say," Rose asked, "has anyone talked to the Parrys lately?"

"They don't know what to do," Dad said. "They don't have any money. They've probably given up hope."

"Well, they need a new attitude," Rose said. "Myles is theirs—and ours."

"Yes, he is," Mum said.

I decided to join them. I briefly checked myself in the mirror and went into the kitchen.

"The dead awakens," Rose declared as I appeared.

"Look," Mum said, standing up, "why don't you go into the living room while I start dinner?"

I sat on the couch, alongside Dad. The street outside sounded full of yelling, screaming and shouted names. I started to wind down after my eventful day and my visit with Myles. Inside my body, my baby seemed very real and alive; I took comfortable in the fact of my pregnancy. It felt good, knowing that a part of Myles was with me all the time. But it also made me anxious, knowing that my child's father was behind bars and that his own family was losing hope, as I had overheard Dad say. He put on some blues music and we sat in the dimming afternoon light. I thought of Norman Rockwell, the American artist who did those paintings of typical Americans. It seemed to me that Dad, Rose and I were in our own real-life Norman Rockwell painting, the three of us relaxing before dinner while listening to music. I looked around and smiled as I absorbed the sight and sounds of that moment: the peaceful faces of Dad, lost in the music already, the soft music in the air. Into this chaos and poverty my child was already, serenely, with us, aware of his or her family. And the child's presence seemed to signal that there was hope for happiness for all of us. I wondered at that instant what our child would look like. I hoped it would be a Myles lookalike, with his height, strength and character. Either way, it would be both of us, since we had both created the child. I knew I mustn't ever forget that.

I thought then of Myles, his face, body, smile and smell and the smoothness of his skin, which I hadn't touched in what seemed like years. I thought also of his lovemaking, the power of his body as he gently brought himself into me, conscious always of my delicacy. He thrust relentlessly and desperately, unable to get inside me deeply enough, unable to love me dearly enough, or to know me personally enough. That same tender energy he shared with me, he put into his work with wood. The wood and I were the two things he loved.

It makes life worthwhile, it really does, when you realize, for the first time, that you are in love and that your love is reciprocated.

"Nedy," Rose was saying, "I'm going to the lawyer with you on Monday." To Dad she said, "Do *you* think he'll want more money?"

"If he does, he does."

"We'll see about that," Rose said.

I wasn't sure what she meant. Rose spends her days working with those difficult people at the community center, so she's much more the psychologist than I am. If Beadle was going to ask for more money, she wanted to be there to sweet-talk him, stare him down or tell him to kiss her ass. Myself, I didn't know if her intimidation tactics, or anything else, would work. Larry Beadle, after all, wasn't born yesterday. Still, he was all we had, or all we could afford, and we had all resigned ourselves to the fact that Myles was in desperate trouble.

Mum called us all in to dinner, which we always ate in the kitchen unless we had dinner guests, but that was rare. We ate in silence and loaded our dirty dishes into the sink. Then she told us all to sit. She reached into one of the cupboards and took out an unopened gift bottle of Grand Marnier she had received years ago, when she was touring as a singer, but was saving for a special occasion. It was one of those funny, unwanted gifts that she had carried around in her suitcase forever. She set it in front of Dad, who looked puzzled for a moment but then understood that she expected him to open it and pour everyone a glass.

Dad frowned, confused. The Grand Marnier was for some sort of special celebration, yet we had just been talking about Myles' legal problems, so what could there possibly be worth drinking to? We had made Myles' problems our own, which they sort of were, mainly because he was my lover and his family seemed incapable of giving him the sort of support he needed. Also, for Dad there was the issue of Myles' obvious innocence, and Dad couldn't stand the idea of a man going to jail for something he didn't do. Especially a Native.

Some news, something profound, was moments away from being announced. He probably wasn't sure he wanted to hear it. Dad didn't like surprises.

Rose caught on quickly enough. She smiled peacefully at Mum and was careful not to look at me. Everybody pretended I wasn't even there. You could have put a cardboard cutout of me in my place and the others wouldn't have noticed.

Mum said, as succinct as always, "Well, this has become a very special and eventful day. Nedy and Myles are going to have a baby. Let's drink to the newest Ignas."

We all sipped our Grand Marnier. Dad took a deep breath, as if from angina or a punch to the solar plexus. "This *is* a surprise. How long have you two..."

"Been in love?" I smiled. "Since the summer."

"A few months, then." He was trying to sort it all

out. But what was there to sort out? What was, was.

I think we spend much too much of our lives trying to justify, rationalize and understand things. Often, it's better not to ponder them too closely, because you will just end up being more confused. But in this modern world of demanding an answer to everything, people just perpetuate their misery. Maybe that's why we're so full of anxiety and despair.

But sharing the news with Dad was easy. The Parrys were quite another matter. They made me wonder and worry. What would Parry himself think of this? He would think, Myles is in jail, he may never come out, jail is an unsafe place and Myles' child may grow up without a father. As if Parry didn't have enough troubles already.

"A few months along," Dad was saying. "Not too

late if you decide you're not ready for this, Nedy. The Women's Health Center is close by."

I glowered at my father. "An abortion? I don't *think* so. It's *ours*, Dad. Myles' and mine—"

"We understand," Mum said. "We're just considering all your options."

"We are all eagerly awaiting the arrival of the newest Ignas," Rose said to me. She knew Dad too well to be offended by what he had said about aborting this fetus. Growing up, she was convinced that he loved me more than he did her. He loved us both equally, of course, but maybe it empowered her in some way to think that he preferred me and maybe she was partly right. I've always seemed unable to find my own ass with both hands, while Rose came across as being more powerful than God, so naturally Dad thought I needed extra nurturing at her expense. Rose was aloof and admired herself so much because she thought Dad didn't admire her enough. Then she started reading books to prove, if only to herself, that she was both beautiful *and* intelligent. Next, she decided it was more important to be smart than beautiful and so she started dressing down so people would pay attention to her mind instead of her face, tits and ass. Rose finally knows herself well; she's comfortable with *who* she is and *why* she is. It mystifies me, though it shouldn't, that she doesn't have a steady boyfriend, though God knows all the guys, and some of the girls, have hot pants for her. I guess most of them are afraid of her, is what it is.

We sat for a moment in silence. The Grand Marnier tasted like orange-flavored medicine, so I poured mine into Dad's glass. He said, "So, we're the only ones who know about the baby besides Myles. Shouldn't we tell the Parrys?"

"Have them over," Mum said.

"One of these nights soon," Dad said.

Mum shook her head. "We'll do it now."

"Now?"

"Now. Call them now."

So Dad went into the hallway to the phone and dialed the Parrys' number. "Hey, Mrs. Parry? Mark Ignas here. Is your hubby there?"

Mum sat there, quite able to hear Dad's loud, exuberant voice. She grinned, knowing that he liked Parry as much as he disliked Mrs. Parry, whom he disliked a lot. Then, "Hey, Parry, how's it goin', eh? Yeah, I'm surviving. You know that Nedy went to see

Myles today, right? Well, she has some stuff to share with you guys, so come on over. Is now OK? You say the women aren't dressed? Well, we're all butt-naked here, too, so don't be embarrassed. Just come over here and we can sit around and talk about Myles and whatever. All right? Good. On your way, if you happen to pass a liquor store"—the nearest one was well out of Parry's way—"it might not be such a bad thing for you to buy a six-pack of Molson's." Click.

He came back into the kitchen with the same smile he always has after talking to Parry. "I guess you overheard. We're going to spring some news on them tonight, eh, Nedy?" he said. "Come give us a hug."

I went over and did just that. I had never felt so loved in my life. That's no exaggeration. My dad loved me and Myles loved me and I was going to have my lover's baby. All I needed was to have my man at my side. If we didn't have much else, we had each other and we had love. Our love sustained us, energized us. Love between Mum and Dad had made Rose and me; love between me and Myles had made the baby that was growing inside me. And now, more than ever, we needed that love to sustain us through the challenges of the weeks and months ahead; for we knew that the future held so many awful uncertainties. And I looked forward to seeing Myles' family in a few minutes. Maybe the visit from the Parrys would spin that love up, out and around, galvanize us in the battle to free Myles and get him back home.

"I wonder if Mrs. Parry and her girls will get all dressed up for us tonight," Mum said. "I can't imagine her stepping outside unless she's checked herself out in the mirror a few times."

"A few *hundred* times," Rose said, cackling.

"Well, we won't say anything nasty when they get here," Dad said.

"That's why they don't have money for the lawyer," Rose said. "Whatever money Parry's Smoke Shop takes in, they spend on clothes. We don't have money for clothes. I couldn't even afford cigarettes, so I had to quit."

"You'd still be smoking if *your* father owned Parry's Smoke Shop," Dad said. "So I did you a favor by not owning a smoke shop."

I tuned them out and thought, strangely, of my first time with Myles. It was inevitable and yet quite surprising. The event awaited us patiently and when it happened, we just went along with it, accepted it as natural and right. It did not occur to us to do otherwise.

Prior to that, I had soaped his back in the shower. I did not deliberately look at his body, his buttocks, or perhaps I did but pretended not to. I was past the point of getting a prurient thrill out of the sight of a male body—my feelings for him were too important for that, too deep. I played doctor with other kids and so did he, I'm sure. We all experimented, and to me it was both very scary and quite trivial. For me, back then, Myles really did not exist as a sexual being—or, rather, he *did* exist that way but that was not the most important part of him as far as I was concerned, so I paid little attention to that aspect of his being.

Myles, too, did not regard me as a female sex object. I was skinny and lacked curves. He did not care; I was beyond judging on a physical level. He loved my soul, as clichéd as that sounds. But certainly we had the capacity to love each other on a sexual level, too, and the moment *had* lingered there for some time, waiting for us to catch up to it.

After one of our dates, Myles walked me home and kissed me goodnight in a way that was not at all brotherly. It was a prolonged, heated kiss, full of yearning. Suddenly he pulled away, as if ashamed of some sort of wrongdoing. He walked quickly home and did not contact me for several days. I didn't know what to think and didn't want to go over to his place to ask him.

He eventually came around. He had with him that mahogany-like statue of the naked man with the muscular torso. Such a beautiful piece of art that he gave to Mum, who at first couldn't believe he had made it himself; she worried that he had boosted it from some fancy art gallery. He seemed all hangdog that day; had he brought over the gift as a way of apologizing to Mum for kissing me days earlier? I could never know with Myles.

After giving the naked man to Mum, he took me out for the day. I felt ecstatic. Myles I saw now was a man, much taller and more muscular with a ponytail and earring but no blue suit and pained smile. He now wore a red-and-black mackinaw and old Levi's with tattered runners. He was the most handsome man alive.

We walked a long way that day. Myles had a slow, ambling walk that said, "Beware." We walked to the bus stop and boarded. The bus was crowded all the way through downtown and into Pioneer Park, and he kept me close. He put his arm around me and looked down at me. His face showed more caring than I had ever seen; his eyes seemed wider and kinder. He smiled and I smiled back, seeing his perfect white teeth and thin lips. The bus bucked and jerked as the driver had to stop because people wouldn't get out of its way, and Myles let out the tiniest grunt of exhaustion. He could look so old sometimes.

It always amazes me to see that Myles has a body, and that I do too—that we are separate beings, although I would like to think otherwise. But each of us is ultimately a stranger to everyone else, and there is nothing one can do about it.

It also amazed me that I was still a virgin. But it should not have seemed so odd to me. I was just waiting for Myles, or for the two of us to grow up enough. He was the one for me, the only one. My virginity was for him to take.

We got off the bus somewhere on Delgado Street

and started walking. It was a weekend afternoon, very crowded, and the people were all young—it was, after all, a young person's street. They frightened me, too, because although they were young they seemed much older and surely knew more about life than I did. At that time the grunge look was in fashion; you wanted to look poor and slovenly if you were middle-class, and these young people walked proudly in their untidy, ill-fitting clothes. They didn't move with the leaden slowness of true poverty; they were bouncy, exuberant, smiling. Young, comfortable and bored, they were fake nihilists, smugly rejecting everything the Establishment represented. But they did not realize that they were actually *embracing* the Establishment, doing as it wished. Like that British punk band the Sex Pistols, whose very nihilism was a harmless charade the Establishment condoned and wanted them to prolong indefinitely because it was an innocuous way of keeping them occupied so they wouldn't become actual nihilists. They were stimulating the grunge economy, which of course was a part of the mainstream economy, and so they were doing exactly as the Establishment wished. I wondered what these fashionable East End nihilists would have thought if they knew the joke was really on them.

Myles looked at me. "Feeling okay?"

I smiled. "Sure. Fine."

"We can do whatever you want. We can walk, rest, eat or get high. Whichever you like."

I was very happy to be there with him but did not like this part of town or the people who inhabited it or the way I felt they were looking at us.

"While we're out this way," I said, "let's just go to Pioneer Park for a while and check it out. I haven't been there since Dad took Rose and me there all the time."

He nodded and we kept on walking. His face was sunny yet mysterious. It was as if he had a treasure—me—and was just waiting till the rest of the world smartened up enough to see how wonderful I was.

We entered Pioneer Park, where there were lots of people, but they were white and looked at us with apprehension because we were Natives. Probably they were afraid of Myles, too. Sometime later, I would have to walk the streets of the city alone and they would ignore me, look right through me, as if I were made of cellophane. I wondered, too, if that was such a bad thing, being looked past and through.

"Pioneer Park," he muttered, looking around as we sat on a bench. "I've slept here a few times, you know. On this very bench."

I let out a small, shocked laugh. "Really? *Why*?"

"Because it was late and I had nowhere else to go. I didn't want to wake my family."

"Why didn't you come to *my* place?"

"You were asleep at that hour, and the Hotel Bayporte's deluxe suites were all booked up. So I had no options left." He grinned and lit up a Player's Light, which he'd probably stolen from his father's store. "I don't have to sleep on park benches anymore, though. I have a puny apartment near here for the time being. I'll show it to you later." He was silent for a moment. "Hey, are you as hungry as I am? Let's go eat. I know of a special place."

So we walked some more, back to where we had started, the Lower East End, then down Main Street till we reached Karma, an Indian restaurant. I had never been there but they knew Myles and teased him about me.

After he went to jail, and I went to visit him during the day when I was becoming hugely pregnant, I sometimes ate at Karma afterwards. Even Jagdeep, who had just arrived from Delhi and couldn't speak much English, urged me to eat. They served me curries and tea and made sure that I cleaned my plate. "Please," they said, "you and your baby must be strong for Myles." They gave me red wine to sip, too. They would stand and watch till I ate, then smile and look after their other customers. "Your little boy," one of the Karma servers said, "will grow big like his father." Their concern sustained me through many difficult times. They were among the very finest people I had met in Bayporte, and they weren't even Canadians. When I grew larger and my mobility was compromised, the delivery guy at Karma would drive me to Bayporte City Jail to visit Myles. He had no obligation to do so, of course, but he did it because he cared.

We had few cares on that Saturday night when Myles and I dined at Karma. We ate and drank and laughed together and were served better than everyone else. "It's OK, we know the owner," Myles said when someone shot us a mean, envious look.

At the end of the meal, we lingered at the entrance and held hands as Myles stood laughing with the Karma server and manager, both men. They all spoke slangy English, and Myles loosened up in a way that he usually did not. His rumbling laughter, and theirs, was hormonal, guttural, testicular. Guy stuff. This was *his* conversation, not mine, and although we held hands, we stood light years apart. I saw, probably for the very first time, how Myles might appear to the rest of the world, and how we as a couple appeared, detached for now from our families. I marveled, that evening, at the respect and affection men can have for one another. Their shared sexual anxiety, their reaction to the domination of women that is such a crushing burden to them.

I have lately thought much more about this, and have concluded that when a woman first observes such male bonding—although, of course, I, at that time, was scarcely a woman and oblivious to most of what occurred around me—she resents it because she is in love with the man doing the bonding and she feels excluded; how else could she feel about it? It is also one of the profoundest things the woman will ever likely see. And in our deeply disturbed world, a woman has no choice but to be intimidated by and envious of this bonding. We probably feel that this bonding is a foreign language we do not and will never understand. But the fact is, whether we like it or not, we are actually *included* in this language, although often we neither realize it nor wish inclusion in such a peculiarly male experience.

I've sometimes felt that when Myles looked at me, he could see the girl I once was, but only because he *wanted* to see her. Men do not have any meaningful secrets from each other, but they have secrets from women that they are too immature to disclose. They mature much later than we do, but not nearly as much, and very slowly, and only with much help from us women. I don't know why, only that it is;

furthermore, it is a terrifying, mysterious thing which is the key to much happiness, or unhappiness, in man-woman love relationships. The man needs to believe he is doing the leading while in reality he is doing the following, being guided by the woman. All the while, he appears to be giving more time, or at least more quality time, to his male friends than he is to her. But men need that camaraderie; it enables them to deal with us and our silence, which for them is inherently incomprehensible. Plus, we, whether we know it or not, are very much at the mercy of a man's imagination; this is the part of him that creates us, and we of course are eager to be created, although most women would vehemently deny this, mainly because we do not realize our desire for this sort of creation. Ironically, a man finds no need or use for a woman's imagination; his alone is sufficient. And in this chaotic life we live, it really is ludicrous to believe, as we have often been told, that women are, or are supposed to be, more imaginative than men. One suspects men are responsible for this fallacy, and I've never known why they would dream up such a notion, especially when you consider that living with a man, and raising his children, and doing all the practical things in life, require little imagination from a woman. Imagination can lead to obsession; obsession and genius may be the same thing. There are no women Einsteins or Mozarts for the same reason there are no female Charles Mansons. The masculine imagination has been responsible for the greatest achievements in art and science. Men have immersed themselves in art and science as a means of escaping women; they've turned to cars and computers and other gadgets.

You can really get confused when you honestly

believe that a man who uses and relies upon his imagination (as the best, and worst, men do) is somewhat less than masculine. It's too bad that imagination is a man's most underrated quality. In our culture, so many of us seem to have one thing in common, which is a desire for money. And if that's *your* thing, the very last quality you need is imagination.

"Let's go to my place," Myles said as we left Karma. "It's a walk, but it'll do you good after that big meal."

"OK, but it's getting late," I said. We started back down towards Davis Street and I felt fine, in need of a long walk. I didn't know the West End then, as I do now, and the newness of it struck me, especially when compared to the oldness of the East End. I'm not sure I would have been comfortable walking along

Davis Street alone. I was tempted to tell Myles I should check in with my parents before heading down to his place, but thought better of it and stayed silent.

His place, as he called it, was essentially a basement apartment on Davis Street. We walked down some steps and he unlocked the door. The inside was cramped and musty; this apartment was smaller than some closets I had seen. The appliances were old, the linoleum scuffed, the ceiling low. Myles had fresh wood strewn about; he didn't care about the interior of his place; he wanted only a workspace. He would happily sleep on the floor and eat out of the sink if, in return, he had a productive day with his sculpting. On top of his refrigerator were two pictures: one of his father and the other of me. We wouldn't spend a long time in Myles' cramped, musty place, but we would remember it forever.

...

Rose buzzed in the Parrys and waited in our doorway as they took the elevator up. I could picture them walking through our narrow lobby and standing in the cramped elevator, muttering their disdain at the fading wall paint and thinning carpeting (their building was no better). Emerging from the elevator to traipse down our hallway, overdressed and perfumed, displeasure at the invitation written on their faces, they would find Rose there to greet them, splendidly pretty in her Save on Clothes business suit, more ravishing than the two young Parry women could ever hope to be. Rose pulled each of these women into a hug they feared would never end, then took Parry into an embrace he wished would never end.

Like all men, he was in love with Rose, and unlike most men, he felt no fear of her.

Mrs. Parry had squeezed herself into a dark-grey dress, losing her struggle to look slim and chic for God and humankind. Her dress was too clingy, her heels too high, her confidence too brittle. God, handsome, judgmental man that he was, surely disapproved of her middle-aged chubbiness. In very small doses I liked her in much the way that I liked bad movies. To me she wasn't a person, she was an event, a spectacle, with her mirthless smile and pretensions. Rose ushered them inside and passed them off to Mum, who after another hug handed them over to Dad, who had his arm around me. Mrs. Parry, being a third of the buck we'd just passed, frowned with resentment, dressed up for no one special and wishing to be anywhere except near us, but what else was new.

Anya and Talia were both my sisters-in-law now. I needed to like them. But I *didn't*, and I knew they didn't like me or their brother. I loved Myles and disliked them for not loving him; and I couldn't see how his sisters, or anyone else, could dislike him, so I also thought they were stupid. They'd never loved nor hated anyone and I held *that* against them, too. So they sat in our living room, our reluctant guests, called over for some mysterious reason. Mum had cleverly furnished the living room with a loveseat and chairs to make it seem larger than it was. Anya, twenty-seven, and Talia, twenty-four, looked at my father with a trace of contempt, seeing his arm around my waist, probably thinking I was too old for such daddy's-girl nonsense. Neither girl had ever been a daddy's girl, and I suppose I held that against them as well.

"So, how's my cocky boy *really* doing these days?" Parry asked me as we all sat. "I just ask because I figure you'll tell the truth, and Myles might not tell me so I wouldn't worry."

Parry looked beleaguered; I could tell how hard he was trying not to break under the strain of Myles' incarceration. But he still managed a smile.

I smiled back. "Myles is coping. He has books to read and lots of time for that, so he's not just rotting away."

"If Myles had done his reading while he was at home," said Anya, "he might not be in jail today."

"Parry," Dad broke in before I made some retort

to Anya. He didn't want a catfight. "Did you remember that six-pack? What did you get, Canadian or Blue? We have pop, too. Diet and regular." To Mrs. Parry he said, "You don't mind if he drinks, right?"

"Even if I *did* mind, he'd do it."

Mum said to Mrs. Parry, "What can I get *you*?"

Mrs. Parry, like all devoutly religious women, was a teetotaler. How had she explained to the other holy-than-thou ladies at church that she was married to the owner of Parry's Smoke Shop? The orders were simple: beer for the men, diet pop for us women.

Rose, leading Talia away by the arm, said, "Come on, girl, let's get the drinks." Talia had no chance to reply or refuse, being afraid of Rose, who was half a head taller. They were a better-looking family than we were—except for Rose, of course. Some people thought she had been adopted. If my baby turned out good-looking, the Parrys would get the credit.

Mum, turning to Mrs. Parry, said, "I can't believe how long it's been since we last got together. It's too bad it's always an emergency or something else that brings us together."

Mrs. Parry nodded. "Yes, I've been running like a fool all over, to see how I could help Myles. I used to know some people in Bayporte who were, you know, *worth* knowing, who could make a phone call or two that might make our troubles go away. But that was years ago. And my doctor says that I must take it easy and not overexert myself because I'm not getting any younger and I want to live long enough to see Myles again. But I don't care about myself, you understand, because I am a Christian and I believe the Good Lord will keep me around long enough to do what he wants me to do." She paused. "I pray all the time and believe that He is just trying to teach Myles the difference between good and bad. Myles hasn't always been a saint, I'm afraid."

Mum had little patience with God talk. "All I can say is, I don't understand Him and His works." Then, "What do you make of our lawyer? It was Rose's idea to hire Mr. Beadle."

Mrs. Parry shrugged. "I don't know. I haven't met him yet. I've been too busy with other things. Parry met him."

Parry said, "Want to know what *I* thought? He's a short, chubby white guy who went to law school and now charges more than the highest-paid prostitute in town. In fact, he *is* the highest-paid prostitute in town."

"Parry, don't talk like that," admonished his wife.

"We may not be keeping him around for that much longer," continued Parry, "if he doesn't make any progress in getting my son out of jail. On the other hand, as overfed white boys go, he isn't the worst or the most corrupt, and that's because he's still kind of young and still has some ethics." He turned to Dad and screwed up his face. "You know I hate the idea of having Myles' life in the hands of some fat little white guy who thinks he's God, but Myles is my only son and I don't see that we have many options. But I guess the world is owned and run by white men, hey? Anyway, there are some pretty evil Asian and Native lawyers out there, too. Lawyers are bastards. Goddamn them all."

"I *hate* that kind of talk!" Mrs. Parry snapped. "It makes me sick! How can you expect Myles to get out of this alive and come home when you're so full of rage? You've got to be optimistic and keep a good attitude. Don't you understand that?"

Mum shook her head. "He's just telling it the way he sees it. He didn't make the world, he just lives in it. He just tries to get by here in the Lower East End, like the rest of us."

"What you need," declared Mrs. Parry to her husband, "is Jesus Christ. Give your soul to Him and all your rage will disappear."

Parry guffawed. "Really? And if I do *that*, will He return my son, safe and sane? Is that how it works?"

Mrs. Parry said nothing.

"I'll tell you this. The day my son walks out of jail

and comes back to his family, I'll become the most devout and loving Christian man you've ever met. *When my son comes home.*" He stood up and walked across the living room and stared down at his wife. "However, if my son is returned to me in a body bag, or he just goes crazy in there and they have to commit him to a mental hospital, I can assure you some people will die in retaliation. Also, I don't want to hear another word about your crucified Jewish boyfriend who died two thousand years ago and how He is going to put things right for us. You love Him more than you love me." He went back across the living room and sat down.

After an awful, prolonged silence, Anya said to my father, "Mr. Ignas? Here we are, as you asked. What now? I assume there's some very important reason for us all being together right now."

"No reason," I said. "My dad called you over just so we could watch your parents fight. There was nothing good on TV, and *my* parents don't fight much and they don't fight well, so we thought it would be fun to sit back and watch *yours* go at it."

"Ha." Anya crossed her arms. "I knew you were dumb, but I didn't know you were mean. I'll never understand Myles' taste in women."

"Anya," I asked, "how many times have *you* visited him? Zero? Why? He starts to wonder if his lovely family is really all that supportive." I paused, but had much more to say, and pressed on. "And what have you told your co-workers about Myles? Do your co-workers at the office even *know* you have a brother? I'll bet you're pretending Myles is still at home, happy and handsome. You're sitting there on the sofa, looking so superior, and I'll bet you have some white boyfriend waiting for you somewhere and you're all pissed off about having to be here with us right now. You couldn't care less about Myles, and everyone here knows it." Mrs. Parry looked at me with murder in her eyes. Parry was trying to fend off a grin.

Anya looked hurt and self-satisfied, as if my outburst were merely further proof of my inferiority. Then, craving a smoke, she pulled out a Player's she had lifted from her father's store and lit it up. She knew how my mum felt about smoking in our home, which was why she did it. Anya was saying, "Fuck you, Ignas family."

Talia and Rose came back with the drinks. They had both overheard; Talia looked embarrassed and Rose looked, if anything, amused, which I expected because I knew my sister's sense of humor. They gave us all cans of diet pop and glasses for the beer Parry had brought over.

All of us looked down at our drinks because we were all afraid to look at anything else. Mrs. Parry looked straight ahead, at the coffee table where Mum had placed Myles' naked-man wood sculpture. Surely she had no idea why such a provocative piece of artwork was in the Ignas' modest living room, any more than she could guess that her own son had created it. How would she have reacted if she'd known he had never considered giving it to her?

I sipped at my pop and couldn't help thinking: *Now I know why these two families don't get together often. Will the baby change anything?*

Talia looked about to speak, her mum shot her a look, and my dad shot me a look that said, *You tell them or I will.*

I told them. "The reason I asked Dad to call you over is to announce something which you will think is either very good or very bad." Dad looked at me with warm eyes. "Myles is going to become a father. I'm pregnant."

I said this to Parry. I expected him to take the news best, to see his eyes twinkle and his lips curl into a delighted o, as if receiving a kiss—*Wow! I'm going to be a grandpa!*—but instead he had an abstracted look, his eyes attaching themselves to some invisible stain on the floor. I thought for a moment that he seemed to take the news as if I had slapped his face with it. He disappeared within himself. No, not yet he didn't; first, he shot the briefest glance at my father, as if seeking a nod of confirmation that this was not merely a put-on, a silly teenager's practical joke—*Your boy knocked me up! Just kidding! Hahaha!* Parry's face *then* became abstracted as he sailed away, into the depths of his own soul, to see who he was and what he must do for his son, for now hadn't he do *something*? But no, there was nothing really for him to do, and my pregnancy was hardly a development of true significance. His son, in the first flower of manhood, had, through quite consensual sexual intercourse, impregnated me, a girl just old enough to buy a drink. But other boys in our neighborhood had impregnated girls far younger—and what of it? The baby, Myles' only way of remaining with us if the very worst happened to him in prison—and the worst seemed likely—could be eliminated in the briefest medical procedure. We had plenty of options, as my father had already noted.

I looked over at Mrs. Parry, whose face was inscrutable and whose eyes were fixed on the coffee table in the middle of the living room. That was where Mum had placed Myles's naked-man sculpture, which she didn't like enough to put somewhere safer (many things on our coffee table had been knocked over and broken).

By and by Parry regained his sentience and raised his glass of beer.

"Mark, this isn't strong enough. Let's go get something else and talk about what's going on." To me, he said, smiling, looking much the way Myles would look in a couple of decades, "Congratulations, Nedy. I can't wait to meet my grandchild. I'm sure Myles can't wait either."

"'Congratulations'?" said Mrs. Parry. "Not the

word *I* had in mind. Tell me, Nedy, who will raise this child?"

"Myles and me."

She cocked an eyebrow. "Is that so?"

Parry, his voice laden with sarcasm, said to his wife, "I guess you could go to that church and pray for Jesus to come down and raise the kid, but I doubt if He would. I hear He's funny that way."

Mrs. Parry got up and walked over towards me, at the other end of the living room. I got up and met her halfway. We faced off. I felt unafraid, having my big sister Rose right there, who, if things got ugly, would be happy to step in and punch out Mrs. Parry. But she looked at me and I looked at her and she began to speak. "I guess you and Myles call your irresponsible premarital sinning love, but that just goes to show

how little you know. These are the days of HIV and herpes; who knows what either of you has been doing with other people? And that baby isn't anything but the devil's work. I hope you miscarry, Nedy, I really do. Any child conceived out of wedlock shouldn't be permitted the privilege of being born and living. My son, unless he rots in prison, will find a better mate someday and have a child worth having." Mrs. Parry held her head up high, telling me off in front of my own family.

Before any of us knew how to respond, Parry got up, went over to his wife and backhanded her so hard that she stumbled backwards, collapsed onto the sofa and blushed as her dress rose above her knees. Her husband chuckled.

Mum gasped. "Parry!"

He chuckled again. "Maybe that'll keep her quiet." To my father he said, "Come with me. I want to talk. I *need* to talk. Hear me?"

Mum pushed Dad at Parry. "Go, go, go." They disappeared out the door, quite happy to be away from this ugliness. Not knowing what else to do, we tried to arrange Mrs. Parry comfortably on the sofa. She probably enjoyed the attention and acted as if she had just had a stroke.

"I really resent what you said to me just now," I told her.

"Don't be so mean," Anya told me. "After all, my mum has bad health problems. Maybe she needs a doctor."

"Yes, she does. She needs a *shrink*," my mum said. To Mrs. Parry she said, "For a Christian woman, you have no Christian values. That baby you were cursing? It's one of us, part of Nedy and Myles. You should stop going to church. You aren't learning anything."

"Now you're mocking Mum," said Talia.

"Oh, shut up," said Rose. "Nedy told me that your mother made Myles go to church all the time but you didn't have to go because you didn't want to. I'll bet *you* mock your mother's faith all the time. I hear that everybody laughs at how that crazy lady carries on at the First Nations Church, using worship as an excuse to get all dressed up and show off for the others. It's like she thinks *she* is going to heaven and nobody else is." Rose sneered at Talia. "You're a bitch. All three of you."

"*You're* a bitch," said Anya. "Mum said what we all felt. Maybe she was a bit harsh, but my father didn't have to smack her. She just asked Nedy how this child was going to be raised, and you got mad at her. Well, she believes in God and goes to church, which is more than I can say for any of you. You're just a bunch of losers. Nedy works at that perfume counter for minimum wage because that's all she's smart enough to do, and Myles is a jailbird who'll never amount to anything even if he gets out, so tell me what chance does that baby have in this world?"

"I'll tell you," I said. "Myles will get out and we'll live happily ever after, OK? And if you ever start up with me again, I'll pound you. Understand?"

Anya laughed and shook her head, which was a dreadful mistake because Rose fixed her with a small, mean smile and spoke without emotion. "Anya, dear," she said, touching Anya's chin with a mother or lover's tenderness, "may I confide in you? Ever since we met, and that was some time ago, I have always admired your beauty. Especially your teeth." At this, Anya's thin, quivering lips widened into the broadest, most terrified smile, exposing those teeth, which were admirable indeed. Both the Parry girls had lovely teeth and nice smiles. "I have *obsessed* over your teeth. Have you ever been obsessed with anything or anyone? Probably not. It's difficult, living with an obsession. Anyway, I have often wondered what you would look like *without* those gorgeous teeth. I mean, if someone just hauled off and knocked those teeth right down your throat, what would become of that beautiful smile? Now, here is my point: if you hassle my sister anymore or touch her, I'm going to find out very quickly what you would look like without those big beautiful teeth. So just go ahead and touch my sister. I fucking *dare* you, bitch."

Anya gulped, hard. She looked about to piss her pants.

No one knew what to say. Rose was a formidable presence, regardless where she was or with whom. Both the Parry girls and their mother found her highly intimidating, even though Rose had never threatened any of them in any way and had always tried to be courteous with them. Now she was terrifying, and the Parry women were unsure of what to do. Hatred seemed as palpable as a pall of smoke in the room. Anya just stood there, speechless. She and Talia were thin women of medium height who knew how to dress to flatter themselves. They were wholesomely pretty women with a mother who had led them to acquire completely unrealistic expectations from life and themselves. Parry's Smoke Shop had put them both through Bayporte City

College, although I couldn't remember what they had studied (perhaps they had never actually told me). One was now an office temp and the other an assistant manager at one of the downtown megaplexes. Again, who did which job? Myles couldn't keep them straight, either.

I was sure they had remained virgins into their twenties, a rare accomplishment in our neighborhood. Their mother had convinced them that they would burn in hell if they had premarital sex. I wondered if they would marry and have families, or if their mother had already damaged them both too much for that.

"Let's get out of here," Anya said, turning haughty. "We're not welcome in the home of these vulgar people." They went to their mother. I could hear their invisible leashes clinking like sad music on the floor.

Their mother felt brazen enough to say, "Mrs. Ignas, it's too bad you didn't raise your daughters as well as I did mine." Mum looked bemused rather than offended, and Mrs. Parry added, "I can assure you *my* girls won't be pregnant till they're married."

"You're talking about Nedy and Myles' child," Mum reminded her. "Yours, mine, ours. One of us. Who cares about a ring or piece of paper? That child is a gift from above."

Mrs. Parry looked ready to say something, but instead just turned and walked towards the door, her daughters just a step behind. I beat them all to the door and blocked their way. "I want to remind you that I'm pregnant with Myles' baby. You may not like that, or you may not like *me*, or you may not like Myles, but that's just how it is. Now you're free to punch me in the belly right now and be done with my pregnancy. Go ahead, I won't stop you. You have had lots of practice killing your own and ruining their lives. Just look at your husband and children."

Mrs. Parry wasn't afraid of me. She simply gave me her coolest, most condescending little smile and said, "We're leaving now, if you'll get out of our way."

"Please, Nedy, that's enough," said Mum.

Rose stepped forward put her arm around my waist and led me over to stand by Mum. "I'll walk you to the elevator," she told our guests.

"We know our way," said Mrs. Parry.

"I'll walk you anyway." When the elevator doors opened and the Parry women stepped inside, Rose held the door. "Look, I can't believe you said those things to my sister. My family are nice people, but I'm a mean bitch. So if when that baby is born, I don't want to see you around here at all, and if you ever even go up to that kid on the playground I will knock *everyone's* teeth out. Understand?"

She came back into the apartment, her face hot with rage. "Guess they won't be back," she said with a bitter little laugh, not at all sure that she had just done the right thing. Normally she prided herself on being restrained, someone who knew just how to handle every situation.

Mum had nothing to say. Neither of us had moved for the past few minutes. We had just stood side by side, mother and daughter, silent and dignified. Now she said, "I think Nedy ought to lie down. The men will be gone for some time." But she really wanted me out of the way so that she and Rose could drink some coffee and talk things over about how the Parry women wanted nothing more to do with Myles, and his father wanted to help but couldn't. My family and I were all Myles had left in the world.

I wandered into the bedroom and concentrated very hard on not thinking about anything at all. Rose, in a very real way, was prepared to carry me on her shoulders till the baby arrived; she wanted this addition to our family as desperately as I did. I crawled into bed and imagined Myles cuddling me as he had so many times, his long arms enveloping me, his breath warm on my neck. I would make him proud of me throughout this difficult time. I would be every bit as brave as he was.

...

In his Davis Street studio apartment, Myles put his heavy wool blanket over me. "Kinda cool in here.

Make you nice and warm." Then he suddenly looked serious, more so than I had ever seen him. The apartment was absolutely quiet, though Davis Street, just outside the door, hummed with activity. I felt fear and exhilaration and a total eagerness for all that awaited us in life.

Myles said, "We're"—he groped for a word—"*adults* now. I never thought I would live this long. Isn't that something?"

"Yes."

"And we love each other, right?"

"Yes."

"And we're going to last forever, right?"

"Yes."

"Can't you say anything other than 'yes'?"

"No." We both laughed, and he motioned for me to come to him. I did, and we held each other and kissed for the longest time. I started to weep. "What's that about?" he asked.

"Don't you know? I always cry when I'm happy."

He stepped away and waved his arms, to include everything we could see. "This is my universe. It's who I am. These pieces of wood are just extensions of me." He picked up a couple of pieces of shapeless wood. "These? I don't know what they'll become. Or maybe *they* do and they just haven't told me yet." He looked at me levelly. "If we make a lifelong commitment, you know I won't cheat on you with other girls, so you'll never have to worry about *that*. And I smoke grass and drink beer, but that's all." He breathed hard; he was telling me that were difficult for him to say, and which I already knew, but it was important, if only for him, to say these things now, so I listened.

"The wood and tools make me alive. I have to work with them as much as I need to breathe. I need a bigger workspace and maybe someday soon I'll have one. So, Nedy, my point is this: I am offering you a very humble life. I don't have an MBA and I'll never drive a BMW because I refuse to wear a suit every day and kiss everyone's ass. So maybe you'll have to work at that smelly perfume counter for the rest of your life, and when you come home I'll be so wrapped up in my work that I'll barely know you're there. But that's the way I am sometimes and I'll have you in my mind all day and night, even if it doesn't seem that way." He smiled. "Is that enough for you, Nedy?"

I said nothing. I just beamed and threw myself into his arms. He led me to his bed and I sat astride him. I could feel his penis hardening through his jeans; he knew I could feel it, and wanted me to feel it, yet was unsure how I would react. He kissed me all over—my face, my chest and shoulders, then lower. I wanted him to do these things, yet they frightened me; I was frightened by what I did not yet understand. I was his now, literally; I liked the idea of being his but the act of *becoming* his somehow unnerved me. Myles was changing me, making me into someone new, and I simply followed his lead and did as he asked, though neither of us spoke. His eyes spoke to me, his heart, his soul. His eloquence was limitless. He kissed me, over and over again, everywhere, his touch at once gentle and powerful.

Then he covered me with the wool blanket and slipped away. The blanket was rough; I wanted to take it off but couldn't. He had disappeared into the bathroom; when he returned, he was naked and wearing a condom. He got under the blanket with me and carefully extended his body over mine. I could feel his long, thick penis erect, smoothly sheathed, against my stomach.

He kissed me hard, several times. "I've been waiting to be here with you," he said. "This will feel so good for both of us. If it hurts, don't worry. The hurt won't last long. Just a minute or two. Then we'll be fine, and we'll have all the time in the world to enjoy each other."

"It's getting late," I said quietly.

"Yeah, nearly four. Don't worry. Your mum and dad know where you are. They won't worry." Then he carefully entered me. "Just relax. Don't worry."

I gripped him and wouldn't let go; I held on,

desperately; he seemed the only thing keeping me from falling off the earth. I grabbed at his ponytail, at his shoulders. He went in, deeper, deeper; one of us moaned, the other cried out; maybe we did both. I wanted him to stop; I begged him to continue. He was taking me to where I had never gone and I wished our voyage would continue forever. His tongue explored my mouth, his hands caressed my body. I stared with wonder at the magnificent wall of his chest, the rippling of his muscles. Just then he moved up but not out and thrust himself into me so hard that I feared he would tear me apart. There was a moment of blinding pain and then none at all. He stifled my silent cries with the deepest kisses, and comforted me with more caresses and moans. His body moved with the relentless power of a locomotive I could not and did not wish to stop. His phallus filled me, made my muscles ache and my breath grow ragged. I wept and giggled and shouted his name, I pulled him closer and sealed his mouth with my own, devouring him till I feared I would consume all of him and there would be nothing left. We kissed and he thrust into me. He ground into me, and I into him, with a terrible violence that frightened and exhilarated us both. The earth shook for us both; the world ended, and we died, and the miracle of life immediately began again. Myles eased out of me and covered me with himself for the longest time.

At last he spoke. "Was it good for you, Nedy?"

I rolled my eyeballs. "Want me to compliment you on your sexual prowess? This was my first time. Maybe I should go do some other guys so I can compare." I wanted very much, at that moment, to know about *his* sexual past. How many partners, who they were, how they compared to me. But I also felt it really was none of my business, and he wouldn't have told me anyway.

Giggling, he pinched my breast. "Don't even *think* about doing other guys." He added, "One thing is for sure. With you around, I won't be needing any Viagra."

We slowly got up together. For the longest time we stared at each other. I looked at him, fascinated by the mystery man who was my lover—the long bronzed body, the thick black ponytail, the well-defined muscles, the formidable flaccid penis. He would remain a mystery to me, of course, forever, both his body and mind, just as each person is always ultimately a mystery to all others.

"Time to get you home," he said. "Your mum is

going to shit a brick when we walk in. It's breakfast time."

So we showered and dressed, all the while kidding each other and grabbing and kissing. He warned me that it would be awkward when he got me home and my mum would bitch and my dad wouldn't be too interested in what Myles had to say to him, and Myles had lots he needed to say to my dad. Myles walked me home; rather, he rode the bus with me, and it was grey outside. The sun wasn't up and it was still dark. We walked the couple of blocks to my apartment building and he said, "Open the door so we can get this thing over with."

He came in with me. My sister was in her bathrobe, waiting for us. She looked so pissed off that you would have sworn she was my mother.

"Hey, Rose," Myles murmured, sheepish.

"Just in time for breakfast," she said.

"Is your dad up yet? Mind if I speak to him for a minute? That's why I'm here," Myles said.

"Yeah, I imagine *he* might want to speak to *you* for a minute, too," she said.

Myles blurted, apparently wanting to practice on my sister before he tried it on my father, "I want to marry your sister."

"Why?"

He let out a nervous laugh, thinking her question was ludicrous, meant to be funny. Presently Mum joined us in the kitchen. She was in her bathrobe, too, looking quite cross. "Do you know what time it is? Do you know how long you have been out on the town? Nedy, I was just about to have you added to that list of 'Bayporte's missing women.'"

"Blame it all on me, ma'am," said Myles. "My idea. I kept the evening going because I didn't want it to end. I had all kinds of things to talk to her about—"

"Just talking?"

Myles blushed the deepest red, caught in a lie. Mum, too, had been young once, partying with boyfriends, staying out all night. Been there, done that. We couldn't have been more obvious to her if we'd come in unbathed, with our underthings reeking of love juice.

"I love Nedy. I want to marry her. She's the only one for me and I want her. There've been other girls but they didn't mean anything. That's why I'm standing here in your kitchen at this weird hour."

Mum looked at me. "How old are you, Nedy?"

"I'm eighteen."

"Do you think you're old enough to know what love is?"

"I know that I love Myles."

"Shit," said Rose. "Isn't the older sister supposed to marry first? If you two marry, I'm fine with that. But why bother getting married? Why mess around with rings and a piece of paper? They can just shack up and screw like everyone else. I'm sure they've already been going at it like nobody's business."

"Thank you for your feedback, Rose," Mum said. "Mark! Get in here! We have some things to talk about."

Dad walked in. He was fully dressed, as if minutes

away from going out looking for me. "I'm sure your mother has already reamed you, but now it's my turn. Do you know what time it is? If you want to keep insane hours, then move out and do your own thing, but don't do it here. Do you know how worried we've been...?"

Myles said, "Mr. Ignas, I apologize for all this. As I was telling Mrs. Ignas, Nedy and I are in love and want to be married. That's why we were out all night—talking about our future. But I told her that you and I need to talk about this thing first, since you're her father and you know her better than anyone else. That's what I came here to say."

Dad looked at him for a long time. "You're twenty-one, Myles?"

"Yessir."

"And how are you going to support her?"

"I won't. It's fifty-fifty. She'll stay at Dunsmuir. But I'm not lazy. I work as a sculptor and do odd jobs. My ship will come in. You'll see."

"So you asked Nedy to marry you and she said yes."

Myles nodded.

"So now you're here. Is this a negotiation or a notification?"

"Sir?"

"Are you *asking* me or *telling* me about marrying my daughter?"

"That depends on your answer."

Dad chuckled. He made a point of looking Myles

up and down a couple of times over. "A sculptor who does odd jobs wants to marry my daughter. Tell me what to do, Myles."

Myles swallowed. He must have felt Dad was mocking him, because his face darkened with anger. "A sculptor who loves your daughter more than anything. A truly good man who would do anything for her." He paused. "Ask the woman he loves. If she doesn't love him back, end of discussion."

Dad turned to me. "Well?"

"I love him with all my heart. I don't care what he does or how much money he makes. I love him for him. To be honest, I really don't need your approval, Dad. But I want it because you're you. If you said no, I would marry him anyway. He's the only one I want."

"When will this marriage happen?"

"We haven't set a date," I said, "but the sooner, the better."

Dad nodded. "You and I better go in the next room and have a little talk, Myles." Done deal. Myles got what he wanted, not that he had ever doubted it. Standing next to Dad, he was the bigger man, an inch or so taller and just as broad across. He had come to ask for my hand, which wasn't necessary, but there was an old-fashioned sweetness to the gesture that touched me and gained Dad's respect.

Mum said, "Nedy, are you sure you want to go through with this? It's a huge step. Forever."

"Mum's only saying that because she was kind of hoping Bill Gates would leave his wife and take up with you," Rose said. "She figured that if you were

Gates's wife, we might actually be able to leave skid row." Mum frowned at the ludicrous joke, but there was an element of truth in what Rose said. Our family did have hopes that one of us would marry someone who could get us out of the neighborhood. Myles couldn't do much for us that way. That left Rose, who frightened big, strong men.

I sneered at her mention of Bill Gates. "That weird little Microsoft dweeb? He's too short and he has a big nose."

Mum chuckled. "I don't think Bill Gates, despite what he looks like, ever had much trouble getting a date on Saturday night." But then she thought carefully about what had been said. Myles, the only boyfriend I had ever had, and the only guy who had ever shown any interest in me, asked me to marry him; his proposal, inevitable as it was, nevertheless somehow seemed genuinely surprising. Or, as I say, perhaps what was surprising was his conventional behavior in coming here to ask my father. If I had simply packed a suitcase and moved in with him, nobody would have thought anything of it.

Mum looked at Rose. "And when are *you* getting married?"

"*I'm* waiting for Donald Trump. He's taller than Bill Gates." Rose smiled sadly. "A hundred men would love to get me into bed, and a few certainly have, but none of them could stand to be married to me and live with me."

Neither Mum nor I knew quite what to say to Rose's blunt, candid admission, although certainly neither of us doubted it was true. We sat in silence; Dad's voice was soft and quiet behind the door.

Soon, the door opened and the men rejoined us.

"It's settled," Dad said, his arm around Myles' waist. "Nedy, I don't know why you two want to make this big step so young, but if you do, you have my blessing." He put my hand in Myles's. "Be true to each other and keep your sense of humor. You'll see soon enough what I mean."

"I'm sure we'll do fine," Myles said, close to tears. "I have to get to my place and tell my dad. I'll call you, Nedy." He impulsively hugged my dad and left, and my dad beamed. My dad didn't often do that; he rarely found things in life worth beaming over.

Later that week we went looking for a loft for him, one that was downtown or close to it. That turned out to be an ordeal, the first of many.

...

My family and I had shopped at Nolan's department store in the Lower East End ever since I could remember. Nolan's, a skid-row institution, developed huge financial problems as the neighborhood declined, and by 1994 it closed forever, taking with it most of the surrounding businesses that had depended on Nolan's for their own survival.

I mention this because, it seemed to me, the failure of Nolan's devastated our neighborhood. I thought it odd it that a department store's failure could have such a dramatic and prolonged impact on an entire section of a large city.

Larry Beadle had his office in a yellowish old building just half a block from the Nolan's building, both of which had civic-landmark status that protected them from demolition. The Nolan's building sat vacant while the politicians argued about what to do with it.

Mr. Beadle, a short man about 40 years old, had a small potbelly and a cherubic face. He seemed personable enough. He had gotten a degree at the University of Toronto, then moved here to attend Northup Law School. He'd begun practicing in this building when Nolan's had kept the neighborhood more stable; he wanted to move his office to a better neighborhood but his lease prevented him from doing so. He reminded us that Myles stood as his top priority; still, I somehow sensed we were just another set of hassles for him, and I hated that feeling. I wanted to like Mr. Beadle but found it very difficult to do so, seeing that he appeared to be the only thing standing between Myles and ten years in prison.

Mum and I sat at his desk and tried our best to

look relaxed and confident.

"Have you seen Myles lately?" he asked me from his padded swivel chair.

"Yes, today."

"He's coping well, I hope?"

I nodded, believing that Mr. Beadle asked about his incarcerated client merely as a courtesy. He surely viewed Myles as our problem, not his. "When we get him home, I'm sure he'll be all right," I said.

"I understand," he said. "But this is a criminal case, and a very difficult one."

I sighed. Mum had warned me beforehand not to antagonize the lawyer in any way. No antagonist here; I had always gone through life trying to avoid confrontations. "I'm sure you're doing your best," I told him.

He smiled and lit a cigar. "A difficult case," he repeated. "And, worse, I have some unsettling news. Mrs. Chu has now left the country. She has moved to Seattle, where she used to live."

"*What?*" I blurted. Mrs. Chu, the woman Myles they had accused of raping, claimed on the record that he had attacked her. So much of our case was built upon the possibility that she might formally admit to having made a mistake in pointing her finger at Myles. And now she'd gone across the line. Myles would rot in jail till she reappeared.

Mr. Beadle nodded. "I was afraid this complicates matters. Bayporte is now filled with painful associations for her, as is Canada. And there's always the chance she'll never return here because she technically is an American citizen. So we have to play the cards we've been dealt, difficult though it is."

"So now what?" Mum asked.

"Well, the legal wheels turn slowly. We wait and see. If I need more money from you, I'll let you know how much. Ideally, she'll have an attack of conscience and come up here to take the stand and say that she isn't sure Myles raped her, but I wouldn't count on that."

"She probably *does* think he did it. Maybe she's convinced herself of it," Mum said. "Seattle. Wow."

"The Emerald City," replied Beadle. "I have to admit that it took *me* by surprise, that she would run off like that. But as I say, she *is* an American citizen, so she is entitled to go down there whenever she wants. The Crown's case will be based upon the testimony of Constable Taylor, who has really the authoritative identification of the suspect. Taylor insists he saw Myles fleeing the scene of the crime, and Mrs. Chu just repeated what Taylor said. Clearly, what we need is to get to her and ask her to return to Bayporte and acknowledge to the authorities that she isn't absolutely, positively sure Myles attacked her."

Mum muttered an oath.

"Seattle is not that far away, June," the lawyer said. "I've sent a private detective to Chinatown, but we haven't been able to get cooperation from her friends here. That's one of the frustrating things about investigating a criminal matter in a multicultural milieu like Bayporte. Here you have Natives, a couple of blocks over there are Chinese, some of whom have just arrived and others were born here, and then there are Indians, Jews and what-have-you. Anyway, none of these groups is particularly eager to interact with each other or with the authorities."

"Can't she be compelled to come back here?"

"Nope."

"If Taylor saw Myles fleeing Mrs. Chu's home, why did he have to go all the way to the Parrys' home to arrest him?" I demanded.

"Nedy, please," Mum said. "But it does sound suspicious, doesn't it, Mr. Beadle?"

He nodded. "Very suspicious. But again, we need Mrs. Chu to admit that she isn't sure it was Myles."

I looked at Beadle, then around his office, an old, creepy place overlooking skid row. Who would have thought I would end up in a lawyer's office, plotting a strategy with this white guy to rescue Myles, who had been unfairly charged with the most heinous of crimes? I couldn't have felt more comfortable if we had been sitting in the Jewish Community Center at the other end of town. But my options were limited. The only thing standing between me and a life without Myles was this lawyer. "It all sounds so hopeless," I said to him.

"Not hopeless. Just difficult." Then, "I truly believe that Myles is innocent, which is why I took this case. I also believe that Constable Taylor is a racist and a liar, a police officer utterly without ethics, and would say so to his face right now if he were standing here. You have said that you were with Myles at his apartment on Davis Street while the rape was occurring across town, and you were with Peter Carter, your friend. Naturally, you are so biased that what you say is meaningless, and Peter Carter is in police custody right now, so whatever he says will have very little importance, too. I need to get in to see him as soon as possible. He's under pressure to change his testimony so that it will be easier to put Myles away. Perhaps this rape is so appalling to the Chinese community that the Crown feels compelled to punish *somebody* and Myles is a most convenient choice. So you see that it will be a difficult road we are on."

Mum nodded.

"I am also hounding the Crown's office to allow me access to Peter Carter."

"What you're saying is," Mum said, "we really need to be patient."

"Yes."

Patience: the ability to wait or endure without complaint. We needed to be patient as we went about our daily lives pretending everything was under control. Myles needed to be patient in Bayporte City Jail as his fate was decided by people who scarcely knew him and were probably absolutely indifferent to him. I needed to be patient so as not to upset myself during pregnancy.

I imagined Myles, just a dozen blocks away, being patient as his ponytail got long and oily. I pictured him scratching all over, dying for a shower and shave, living with me in his mind and groin. He was there because people had lied about him, and if the lies continued he would remain there indefinitely, living in the stink of other men, doubtless defending himself against their sexual advances. But what was he to do; how could he manage his own rage?

Patience was a luxury we could not afford. We did not have whatever currency it accepted. Myles would wither and die in jail. There, in Larry Beadle's law office, I burst into tears.

"Come now, Nedy," said Beadle, because he could think of nothing better to say.

Mum took me into her arms and held me tightly. She whispered, "Don't do this. Do you hear me? Don't do this. Not here." After a few more seconds of helpless sobbing, I felt myself being gently pushed away by Mum. "Nedy, you're an adult now. Soon, you'll be a mother. You're old enough now to understand that challenges in life are meant to make us stronger. You can't just cry and pretend that they'll go away or that someone else, like me, will magically make them go away. We're Natives; we've been fighting for our rights and lives for a long time now.

We can't stop now. We have to press on. We need Myles out of there and back home, and *he* needs *you* to stay strong for *him*."

I nodded and blew my nose. Mum said to the lawyer, "May I have that Seattle address for Mrs. Chu?"

"Yes." He handed her a computer printout. "This is her apartment's address. She's there as we speak."

"That was quick, tracking her down." I said

Mr. Beadle grinned. "It's called computer technology, Nedy. All the information you need instantaneously. You can run but you can't hide." His state-of-the-art laptop computer sat glowing and humming on his desk. His office still smelled a bit musty from the dust of decades of previous tenants. This building, like so many others, was so old that it was protected by civic-landmark status and nobody could tear it down.

"Will you get in to see Peter soon?" Mum asked.

"Tomorrow, ideally. I'll keep bugging them to let me in. He's where Myles is, but in another section."

"We'll start putting the next payment together tonight," Mum said, "and I'll get Rose to call you tomorrow to let you know when to expect it."

"That would be fine. Give Rose my best." Turning to me, he said, "Nedy, when I go to see Myles, he's going to ask how you're doing. I'm an ethical man. I never lie. What should I tell him about you?"

"Tell him I'm fine."

"*Are* you?"

"Yes."

He smiled. "All right, then."

We thanked Mr. Beadle for his time and left the building to walk home down Waverly Street, where we had lived all our lives and where people like Larry Beadle would never live, a place now full of vacant stores and grungy loiterers who lived only for their next fix.

. . .

I can picture Myles walking down the street when he is reunited, quite by accident, with his boyhood friend Peter, who, unfortunately, has changed very little from the oversized, boisterous kid he had been. After some bear hugs and high fives, the two go into the Astoria, Winton or Eisenhower hotel bar, it doesn't matter which one. Myles doesn't particularly like any of them.

"Are you still living nearby?" asks Peter, his eyes wide and his voice full of wonder at meeting up with Myles again. Life is a funny thing; you can be friends as kids, remain in the same neighborhood as adults and never see each other again. Or you might even have put the other person out of your mind years ago, then bump into him one day and renew your friendship.

Myles said, "I live on Davis Street now. Got a small apartment."

Peter laughed. "For real? I've been here all along, too, and we never bumped into each other. That's too weird. So, guy, whatcha been doing?"

"Keeping out of trouble, mainly. Getting married soon."

"Married! No shit? Who's the lucky girl?"

Myles smiled. "Nedy."

Peter frowned. "Nedy?"

"Yeah, skinny little Nedy. Don't tell me you don't remember her. She's been my girl since day one." Then, "So what's up with *you*? Working at all?"

Peter chuckled. "Got a janitor job through one of those Native employment services. Not what I had in mind, but it helps pay the bills."

"How's the family?"

"Oh, my dad died a few years back. I live with my mum. She's driving me nuts. I can't wait to get my own place. Just working for now and trying to keep a good attitude."

"You have to go anywhere right now?" Myles asked.

"Right now? At this very moment? No."

"Then come with me to my place on Davis Street. It's a lot better than this funky little bar. Nedy's there right now. She can make us something to eat."

Back at Myles' apartment, they sat at the kitchen table, nursing their beers. Peter said, "So, you two are gonna tie the knot, hey?"

"Yeah, I have a lot of things going on. We're looking around for a loft so I can work better. This little apartment is much too small. Maybe they have what I'm looking for in Gastown, as long as it doesn't cost too much. There are probably lots of lofts in Gastown that nobody wants because it's so noisy and freaky at night, with all the drugs and hookers." They are both sitting at the cluttered kitchen table, sipping on their cans of Molson's. "But you know that they sure don't like Natives around here, and they're really going to hold that against me. Sometimes we go looking at those places together, sometimes I go alone, sometimes Nedy goes alone. But from now on I'm going to have to be there because not long ago she went alone and the landlord thought, you know, there's this little Native girl all by herself, and you know how horny those Native girls are. So Nedy says to me, 'I found you a loft! Can you believe it?' But then I went over there with her and he saw me with my long hair and attitude and he said, 'Sorry! There's been a mistake! I promised the loft to someone else.' I called him a lying sack of shit. He thought I was going to pound him one and said, 'If you don't leave right, I'm calling the cops." Myles paused. "But you see, I have it all figured out now. The best thing to do, I've decided, is to win a lottery and just leave this country, period."

Peter said, "You mean, like, go to the States?"

"No, that's worse than here. Besides, Nedy and I can't speak American." The two laughed.

"Maybe you could leave the country by yourself, find a new place to live and send for Nedy later."

"Couldn't do that either. I don't want to be away from her for more than ten minutes at a time."

"Don't you trust her?" Peter asked.

"It's not that I don't trust *her*, it's that I don't trust the rest of the male population. Nedy is so damn friendly, all smiles, and there are lots of guys who'll look at that smile as a come-on. Well, I'm a guy, so I know what guys are like." Myles sips at his beer. "It's taken me this long to figure out what I have in life. I have my work as a sculptor, and I have Nedy. That's it, man. There's nothing else. If I lose those two things, I have zero."

"Well, you have plenty more than I do, so I envy you. Say, you got another beer?"

Myles nodded at the refrigerator. "Yeah, help yourself."

Peter popped open a can of beer and took a long, greedy drink. "You know where I've been the past couple of years? Prison, man. They charged me with auto theft, even though I can't even drive. But I had some pot in my pocket, so they got me for *that*, too. I would like to see the car I supposedly stole. I hope it was something worth stealing, like a Trans Am." He paused and shook his head, as if still unable to believe what had happened to him. "Maybe I'd feel better about this if I had actually stolen something and got caught. Two years of my goddamn life for auto theft!"

Myles just nodded and listened. He put his hand on Peter's neck and let it remain there for a moment. "Take it easy, guy. How long ago were you released?"

"A few months."

"And you're still in one piece. You're still sane and young. You have a job. Things could be worse, a lot worse, and you need to look at it that way."

Peter shook his head. "But *you* weren't there. I was. The things I saw in prison! I was terrified. I wouldn't wish that on my worst enemy. And all because there was a car reported stolen, and they needed a fall guy."

I said to them, "You guys hungry?"

"Bet your ass we are," said Myles.

To me, Peter said, "You look pretty good, Nedy. Haven't gained two pounds since we met."

"That's called not getting enough to eat. And since I'm going to be marrying a starving artist, I probably won't be getting fat."

"Well, maybe that's one of the benefits of marrying a starving artist," Peter said.

"Yeah, and you don't get diabetes, heart disease and all those other fat-people problems," I said.

"You sound like quite an authority on medical matters. Did Myles teach you everything you know?"

"I taught *him* everything *he* knows."

"Well, I always knew there was something special about you, but I could never quiet figure it out."

"So now you know: I'm a genius."

"God, would you just listen to her?" Myles said. "Sometimes she sounds so stuck-up that I just want to slap her around. Maybe that would shut her up."

"How does that corny old song go?" I said. "'Lord, it's hard to be humble when you're perfect in every way.'"

We all laughed, and Myles said, "I guess you just need to take life one day at a time. Otherwise, you'll never make it through."

"And if you don't stop talking and start eating, you'll never make it through dinner," I say. I have made a seafood pasta dish, one of the easy-to-prepare meals that Myles likes.

"Best meal I've had in ages," Peter says, scarfing down the food. "Mind if I move in? I won't take up that much room and the two of you can take turns picking on me all you want."

Myles nods. "Let's do it. Nedy will never make the cover of the fashion magazines, but she certainly can cook up a storm."

"Well, everybody has something special they can do," I say, and the three of us chuckle and keep eating. It's always nice to be appreciated, and I've always taken a certain amount of pride in my sense of humor.

Myles devours a second helping. Peter and I, unaware of just how hungry we were, shovel it down, too. Myles and I beam at each other with our eyes glued to our plates; we are probably roaring with silent laughter, too, to which Peter is oblivious. Or perhaps he knows, or suspects, that we are beaming and laughing, though not at him. We have escaped from the world and found privacy here in the Davis Street apartment. We are happy to share, for a few hours, with Peter; he probably doesn't begrudge us our happiness because if *we* have found some, maybe *he* will, too. His optimism, which may not last long, gratifies me.

Peter enjoys his visit so much that, at midnight, he is reluctant to leave. Myles insists on walking him to the bus stop. Peter fears adulthood yet resents his mother for encouraging him to remain a child. He seeks independence but is paralyzed with fear by the implications of self-sufficiency. Myles, a couple of years younger, feels awkward playing the older brother, dispenser of wisdom and empathy. But he knows, and refuses to ignore the fact, that Peter, literally, has no one else to turn to.

. . .

At the bus stop, and on many subsequent occasions, Peter tried to relate to Myles the horror his experiences in prison. Sometimes he did so at the apartment, while I was there; other times, he spoke to Myles alone. Often, during these times, Peter burst into tears and needed to be held, by Myles or me. He spoke of what had happened to himself, reluctantly and with much mental violence, as if performing an exorcism on himself.

"They came right to my door, the cops. I didn't know why, though maybe I should have. The cops know me, they know my friends, and some of my friends shoot heroin and smoke crack. Bayporte's a big dope town, right? And our neighborhood is full of it all the time. You see a Native guy down here, there's a good chance he's high or at least he has some shit in his pocket. Then the cops, they go to the police station and say, 'We're fighting the war on drugs, sir. We just caught this guy with marijuana.' So they look good and the newspapers are running stories about it and the public thinks we're winning the war. And you know I'm not bullshitting. That's the way it is."

I shrug. I don't know anything about all this. I'm just Nedy, who smells of perfume all day at Dunsmuir. But Myles knows too much about all this, so he stays quiet and listens.

"So I had this bag of pot in my pocket, and when they searched me, my blood ran cold and I knew how much trouble I was in. I thought of screaming for my mum, who was just inside our apartment, but what good would that have done? She would have just worried. So they took me down to the station and the wheels of justice started to turn. They put me in the holding cell with these other guys that I would have avoided on any dark night, and you could tell they had been through this kind of shit before and didn't really think much of it, it wasn't anything they couldn't handle. Streetwise. And I just sat there, bad and tough and mean, like I knew what was going on too and wasn't about to take all this too seriously. I thought of calling my boss, but this wasn't his problem and I don't think he would have been in a big hurry to help me out. So I figure it's my problem and I have to get myself out of it.

"There's this old guy in the cell with us, he's pretty far gone—crack, heroin, booze, he's been at it for years, you can tell just by looking at him—and he's puked all over himself. So he starts *singing*, right? I'm not sure why...and some of the other guys in the cell, they're coming off dope and they're starting to shiver and moan. These guys are no older than I am and they're really hurting, but I can't do a thing to help them, and the cops here, who can see he's sick, they *won't* help him. I bet they were enjoying it, seeing him sweat like a pig and writhe around in that cell. Probably no cop in the world can get it up unless he sees some poor bastard suffer.

"I'm no addict, so I didn't get sick, but I had to shit so bad I was starting to sweat. But they weren't going to let me till they were damn good and ready, so I had to hold it in. I'm surprised I didn't die of a heart attack, holding it in for that long."

Peter grinned. "That's all I can tell you for right now. There's a lot of stuff I probably will never be able to say to *anyone*."

I didn't tell him that it wouldn't make any practical

difference if he told us, anyway. During these cathartic sessions he needed to be held, although often he didn't want it. I held him, when he could stand to be held, and Myles did, too. We were, it seemed to me then, the only people he had in the world. Which, ironically, made him luckier than many others, who had nobody at all.

...

The day after my visit with Larry Beadle, I saw Myles promptly at six-thirty. He looked so distraught that I nearly tried to smash through the Plexiglas and take him in my arms. Whatever glue had held him together was coming loose.

"Why isn't the lawyer doing more to help me out?" he demanded. "With computers and the 'Net and all that shit they can use to figure out crimes, an innocent man shouldn't have to rot like this."

"Mrs. Chu has gone to Seattle. We'll try to get her to come back up here."

"Yeah? When?"

"Soon. We'll go down to Seattle, if we have to."

"Seattle's a big place. And maybe she went to California or New York." He sneered. "Maybe she went to Timbuktu or Mars."

"Myles..."

"Maybe the Crown's office paid her way."

"I doubt it."

"I wouldn't be surprised if they did. Anyway, wherever she is, how will you track her down?"

"We've all got jobs. We're all saving a bit of

money."

"'Send lawyers, guns and money, 'cause the shit has hit the fan,'" he sang in an angry tenor. It's one of his favorite songs. "Well, somehow I don't think my father is going to sell enough crack pipes and *Hustler* magazines to get me out—"

"Myles!"

"What?" His eyes narrowed, his lips were white with anger. "I just wanna know what the fucking lawyer is doing besides jerking off all day while I rot in this goddamn jail. I can't eat the fucking food and I can't sleep. I'm dying in here and nobody gives a shit!"

"I do."

Myles sat back and sighed. "I'm sorry. I shouldn't take it out on you. I guess you're all trying hard to help me out, but it doesn't do any good." Silently he screamed, *"Get me the fuck out of here!"*

"Just be cool. Remember, there's someone here who loves you." I patted my stomach. "Two of us, in fact."

He smiled in spite of himself. "How long now?"

"I'll start showing more next month."

"So, which do we want? A boy or a girl?"

I shrugged. "Doesn't matter to me, as long as it's healthy and beautiful."

"I'm sorry I lost it a minute ago, Nedy. But you know how it is for me."

"I know."

"I gotta get out of here."

"Yes. We're working on it."

"Give me a kiss." We pressed our faces against the Plexiglas and puckered. "You still love me, right?"

I smiled. "Of course."

"Even when I'm an asshole?"

"*Especially* then."

The guard came up and said visiting hours were over. Myles just turned away and walked with him. I left the room and returned to the no-man's-land that was home, sweet home.

...

That night, and on others, I dreamed that Myles was at the Great Elizabeth Exhibition's fairgrounds, on the roller coaster we'd ridden many times before it was dismantled and removed. Myles sat all alone on the roller coaster; in fact, there was nobody else on the vast fairgrounds. Myles, terrified as he grasped onto the bar, screamed for me to throw the switch so he could get off. But I could not find the controls anywhere, and when Myles, shooting past me, pointed frantically at an area past me, I found a white man hunched over the controls. I begged him to stop the ride, but he paid no attention to me. In fact, he didn't even move. Sometimes I actually jumped onto his hunched white back and discovered that he was made of wood. Then I woke up to find Mum standing over me with a cold towel, her face full of concern.

"There's nothing I can say to you now that will help ease your mind. I can't promise you that your suffering will end anytime soon, because I have done my share of suffering and know that it ends when it ends. Things may turn out well where Myles is concerned, but they may *not*, too, and you need to prepare yourself for that. A lot of innocent men have gone to prison, and Myles may never get out of there. That's the fact. If that happens, it will be more important than ever for you to bring his child safely into this world. You need to be tough, now and always, but don't harden yourself to the point where you feel nothing at all. Grief is better than nothing. Understand?"

I just said, "Yes, Mum," because I didn't know what else to say, was too exhausted to say anything else and knew she didn't expect me to say anything more. Besides, I lacked the strength to speak, think or move, but I was going to have to find some strength. And soon.

"OK now? For the time being?"

I nodded, and Mum said, "Just remember that love has enabled us to survive life so far, because we haven't had much else going for us. So don't give up on love."

. . .

I did not sleep. I stared at nothing in the darkness, thinking of Myles's face, his silent scream: *Get me the fuck out of here!*

I thought about women I had seen working the streets throughout my neighborhood, glassy-eyed, lacquered-up chippies ready to do business. They scared me. I thought they looked at me with contempt, or maybe I was contemptuous of them. They were selling their bodies for money; one commodity in exchange for another. I now knew that my contempt had nothing to do with their illicit streetcorner presence. It was the low value they placed upon themselves that angered me, and the degradation to which they submitted themselves. I could not imagine myself on the streets, offering myself, in my own neighborhood, as just another piece of Native ass.

But how much was Myles worth to me?

Grey light crept through the blinds as I finally nodded off. My alarm clock buzzed not much later and I awoke, muzzy and aching. I thought at first of calling in sick, but decided against it. Dunsmuir needed me so its customers could sniff my wrist all day.

I got dressed and joined Mum for toast and tea. Dad and Rose had already left. I was too tired to speak, so we ate and drank in silence. I had many thoughts rushing through my head, but could not have spoken to Mum about them. Maybe that was for the best.

I left our building and walked to the bus stop at Waverly and Haber. The overcast morning sky depressed me. Across the street, the homeless people who'd camped out in front of the community center all night milled about. At the Winton, Regent and Eisenhower hotels, sleepless crack addicts fidgeted in their dingy rooms. I wondered, perhaps for the hundredth time: What had gone wrong for these people? Who were they? Discharged inpatients from the psychiatric hospital, probably, without medication or even a bed; the luckier ones got squalid rooms at the weekly hotels and an occasional visit with a shrink. In a few hours, the Mexican drug dealers would arrive from the suburbs, dressed in Canucks caps and denim jackets, squawking on cell phones or accepting money from addicts right by the community center's front steps. I told myself that if I was going to turn tricks, I should probably go to another part of town. I could make money by doing a second legitimate job, but hooking, while dangerous, would be more lucrative. I also told myself what I was afraid of even thinking: that I would have to wait till the baby was born, and if Myles wasn't home by then, the decision would be a no-brainer.

I boarded the bus and stood, butt to butt, with all the suburbanites on their way to Financial District jobs. I smelled lots of perfume and cologne and felt the stares of professional people who looked at me and saw a Lower East End Native girl, dressed up, and looking so tired first thing in the morning. God knows what they thought I had been doing all night to look so haggard first thing in the morning.

I also thought about the weeks ahead, and how I would manage to get to work as the baby in my belly grew. If I passed out on the bus, I couldn't count on these people for help; they would just sneer at me and stomp on me. If I was lucky, they might step over me, if only for fear of ruining their good shoes. And, who knows? By the time I started to show, Dunsmuir might decide that having an unmarried, obviously pregnant teenager at the perfume counter just wouldn't do and it would be goodbye, Nedy. *Myles may never get out of prison. If that happens, it will be more important than ever for you to bring this baby into the world. Understand?*

I stood inside the crowded bus and sighed. For some reason, buses had always reminded me of a sort of prison cell where the inmates wore fancier uniforms. The man next to me, having trouble with his potbelly, leaned into me without apology, then righted himself. He looked at me without seeing me, and breathed on me, his breath scented with liquor even this early. He was probably contemplating how he would get through the morning without another drink.

The bus lumbered onto Grand Street and I got off in front of Dunsmuir. I entered the employees' entrance, punched in, washed my hands and hurried out to the perfume counter so that the manager could spray my wrist with that day's scent, which usually smelled way too much like the gooey soap I'd just used. He checked his watch, saw that I was two minutes late and winked at me.

As I say, it's mostly white women and Chinese women who shop here and smell my wrist. But sometimes a Native woman will come in, too, looking with amused disbelief at the price tags on the suits, watches, wallets and whatnot. Maybe she will wander over to my department; seeing me, she will wonder why I'm there, or maybe she surmises that I'm the token Native. You don't need a marketing degree to know that I'm certainly not representative of that store's customers. If she asks about that day's scent, I'll give her my wrist to smell; if she wants her own wrist sprayed, I'll sweetly explain that I can't do it because the perfume costs too much. Male customers frequently aren't shy about sniffing my wrist and trying to turn it into some sort of zipless fuck, brushing their lips against my wrist for the longest time while gazing into my embarrassed eyes. Just another day at the office for me.

Rose met me that day because we had things to

discuss; the manager invited her inside as they locked the doors. She cut quite a smashing figure in her grey overcoat and short haircut, silver-dollar brown eyes and movie-star smile. There was a certain softness in her face that disguised her tough personality and made the Dunsmuir management wish she worked there, selling cosmetics to women who would have killed to look half as good as she did. All my co-workers were in love with her, even the homosexuals.

Outside, as some of the passersby were giving her a prolonged, admiring once-over, she reminded me that the woman at the center of our mess, Mrs. Chu, was in Seattle, and someone had to go down there and come back up here with her. Rose wanted to go into the mall and buy me a cup of coffee because she had these things on her mind.

"The lawyer's coming too, right?" I asked above the rush-hour din of Grand Street.

"Did he say he would when he gave Mum Mrs. Chu's address?"

"Well, not exactly."

"Then, no. This is *our* problem, not his. Besides, Beadle has to stay here to deal with the Crown prosecutor and that racist cop Taylor."

"But we don't *know* Seattle," I said. "How are we going to get her to come back up here?"

"As I said, we have a problem." Then, "Let's just sit down somewhere and talk this thing through."

Big sister Rose, taking care of business as usual. At such times I remember how much she loves me and how she chooses to express her love. I also can't believe that she is just a few years my senior. How did she get so worldly?

...

Mrs. Mooi Lai "Barbara" Chu, an American national residing as a landed immigrant in Bayporte, states that on the evening of February 15, she was at home in Bayporte's Chinatown when a Native male forcibly entered the premises and sexually assaulted her. She positively identified her assailant as Myles Robertson Parry.

I wouldn't know Mrs. Chu if I bumped into her in a won ton house. Beadle discovered that she was born in Hong Kong and moved to the States as a child, became a citizen and divorced her American husband to marry a Chinese Canadian who had lots of money. He also had a gambling problem and a secret girlfriend, but at first things were OK between them. She was separated at the time of the alleged sexual assault; her husband has his own place in another downtown neighborhood while she has a Gore Street apartment in Chinatown. It was from this apartment that Myles fled, according to Constable Taylor, who just happened to be in Chinatown at that particular moment.

...

Rose and I went into Grand Street Mall and settled into the Thirsty Limey, a big, dark restaurant and pub known for mediocre food, indifferent service and 200 brands of beer. We just ordered coffee and Rose tapped on the round wooden table, as she did whenever she had a lot on her mind. Her way has always been to get straight to the point; she has no use for small talk, and I don't especially like her style. But she's always had her own way, and this time things weren't going to be any different.

I had been considering working the streets to raise money for Myles' defense. While I wasn't about to tell Rose, I did say, if only to make conversation, "Do you think they'll find the rapist?"

Rose rolled her eyeballs. "Who knows? Who cares? Myles is in jail, and that's the only thing that's relevant." She sipped at her coffee, her voice quiet but her body tense and agitated from the visit with Beadle. "I'm sure she probably was, and the rapist was smart enough to pull out his thing to prevent a DNA identification. Then she called the cops and here we are."

"Then how did all this get pinned on Myles?"

"They had a rape complaint, they assumed one of

ours did it, so they hunted around the Lower East End for some young Native guys. Maybe Myles had given Taylor some attitude once or twice. The cops needed a suspect and she just wanted to see someone get punished, so they found Myles and said, 'Is he the one?' and she was, like, 'Yeah, I guess that's him.' Anyway, that's my theory. Mine and Beadle's."

"So, we go down to Seattle and politely ask Mrs. Chu to come back to Bayporte with us and change her testimony. She'll say it wasn't Myles, or she isn't sure if it was. And that's the best we can hope for."

Rose nodded. "Pretty much. I don't know how we'll talk her into coming up here, either. Plus, Peter can tell the truth, that he and Myles were together when the alleged rape took place, but Peter's been in prison and his word Ignas zero."

"That cop Taylor is responsible for all this," I said.

"Beadle started a file on him. Taylor is a rock star"—a crack smoker. "That's why he was in Chinatown. One thing Constable Taylor got from working a Lowe East End beat, besides a crack habit, was a cheap and reliable source of drugs. Nice, eh?"

"I thought how nice it might be to borrow Parry's revolver and blow Taylor away."

My sister smiled. "Well, I don't think that would be an option, although it would provide a certain satisfaction."

"Now, about Seattle..."

"Right. That's why I called this little meeting. You, obviously, can't go. We need your Dunsmuir paychecks and Myles needs your moral support. *I* can't go because I make much better money than you do and I need to keep Beadle motivated. *Dad* can't go because he wouldn't know what to do or say and Parry is even less diplomatic. So guess who it's gonna be?"

"Mum?"

"Mum."

"But she doesn't know Seattle," I said.

"And she's the last person in the world who would want to do this. She hates Greyhound buses, too. But she has the street smarts to pull this off. She can persuade people."

I shrugged. "What do you think about Peter? Will he be much good to us when he tells the jury that he was with Myles when the rape took place?"

"Beadle is meeting with him tomorrow. That doesn't mean a whole lot, of course. Peter can swear he was with Myles when Mrs. Chu was raped, but it doesn't mean anything. Nobody would believe him."

"Situation FUBAR," I said. Rose smiled. She'd taught me that FUBAR meant Fucked Up Beyond All Recognition. She'd learned it from the regulars at the community center.

We fell silent for a few minutes in the dark coolness of the Thirsty Limey. After work, the Howe Street yuppies liked to go there to brag and bitch to each other and many of the customers seemed to be eyeing us. I pondered what they made of us, two fancy Native women, dressed up and perfumed, sitting in a place like that among all those horny young white men. They probably did not know we were sisters because, alas, we looked absolutely nothing alike; I guessed they took us for a lesbian couple or prostitutes. If we were the latter, why hadn't anyone given us the eye? Rose was the cutest chick in town.

We took turns staring at our coffee cups. For the first time that I could remember, Rose seemed to encounter a problem she couldn't solve. Busing Mum down to Seattle to talk Mrs. Chu into coming up here for Myles' sake struck me as an exercise in futility, and therefore Myles was doomed to a lengthy prison sentence. I was ready, almost, to give myself over to despair when, lighter than the gentlest tap, I felt my unborn baby's kick, just a little flutter in the vicinity of the rib cage but it reminded me, or perhaps the child reminded me: "Hey, *I'm* here too." There were some things greater than ourselves.

The baby wasn't ready to meet the world yet, but

soon it would be. It was preparing for that huge moment, and I had to prepare too, for the birth plus all the other things that were happening in my life, because these things would happen regardless of my preparation.

"Let's get busy," I said to Rose.

"Let's."

. . .

Elsewhere, blocks away, Dad and Parry sat in a bar not far from home, resolving our issues in their own way. Dad, obviously, in this whole mess felt somewhat better off because his kids were free, and he'd never had a son. He'd wanted one, certainly, and doubtless felt disappointed when Rose, then I, came along, but maybe he'd never realized the dangers of having a son in the Lower East End, and only now, because of

Myles, did he realize his good fortune. While he considered this his problem, it was much more Parry's. Dad knew it was luck, and luck alone, that allowed his daughters to turn out as well as they did, and Parry's luck had been less. Empathy and brotherhood compelled Dad to help Parry as much as he could, certainly, but there was also the realization that the two of them were in this predicament together.

Dad and Parry were now middle-aged family men who looked at each other with the belief that their predicament would almost surely have a tragic ending.

Both men looked better than their ages and lives would have indicated. Dad had always looked to me like a Native Bill Cosby, with a broad, funny nose, quizzical features and a face full of whimsical good humor, which made me question his effectiveness as a security guard.

Parry, unlike Dad, was conventionally handsome, an older version of Myles. He had the chiseled dark-red skin of an extra in some John Wayne cowboys-and-Indians movie. His eyes were long and narrow, his face serious but with more than a hint of vulnerability.

Dad watched as Parry sipped at his beer. Then Parry, full of bitterness, said, "Well, if you've come up with some great idea lately on how to get my son out of prison, I'd sure love to hear it."

"I have an idea or two. Our main thing is not to get so angry that we can't think. Rage paralyzes you, and a paralyzed man isn't much good to himself or anyone else."

"Don't forget about money," Parry says. "We need to come up with ways of getting some bucks together."

"What does money have to do with this whole mess?" Dad asks.

"Everything."

"And when was the last time *you* had money?"

Parry shrugs.

"No money, but you're still here," Dad said. "You and your family aren't starving. Money has never meant *that* much to you, so why is now any different?"

"This *is* different," Parry said.

"The hell it is. Do you think that money has anything at all to do with whether or not Myles gets out of jail? Is that what you believe? Well, that's exactly what the white men in power want you to believe, and if you start believing it, he's *really* got you." Dad takes a deep breath. This is his favorite subject, although I wish it weren't. "What is shocking to me is that the white man has tried, for two centuries, to annihilate an entire people, and all the while this execution has been happening the American and Canadian governments have pretended nothing was wrong and the white people have been going on about the governments' commitment to life, liberty and the pursuit of happiness. How can the white government and the white people sleep at night when they have been strangling the life out of the only indigenous culture this whole continent has? They have shot, stabbed, maimed and raped us and kidnapped our children. The encyclopedia says there were 10 million Natives when the white man first arrived, and now there are about one million. *One million!"*

Parry shakes his head in disgust as Dad continues. "Our ancestors owned all the States and Canada, and now what do *we* have? Our shitty little apartments in Canada's poorest postal code. We were independent, but we have nothing now. Whenever a white man wanted a piece of land from a Native, he took it. He took all the river valleys, all the fertile land...shit, what *didn't* he take? He left us with memories, and bitter ones. The government took the land with the military or with documents and promises. The white man lied, cheated, stole, defrauded. They ripped us off, period. They swindled us and now they say they didn't. But they *did* kill, maim, torture. They did the most despicable things that one people could do to another. The governments today will not admit or recognize it as theft or fraud. Our kids went to school and do you know what their history textbooks said about this whole outrage? Nothing! Or maybe two paragraphs that made it sound like we happily gave up this land to them and looked forward to working together. The relationship between the American and Canadian governments with the Natives is unprecedented in history. It's worse in the States. Has any other country, anywhere, made as many treaties, promises, statements and agreements in order to acquired land, then *ignored* those words and documents as if they didn't exist? Those bastards had no intention of honoring their promises to us! Four hundred treaties, and not one of them held up! It's outrageous and shocking, and a *hell* of a lot more important than the NHL scores or any of the other trivial shit we spend our time talking about."

Parry nodded and said, "Well, exactly what do you

206

want *done* about it?"

"I want us Natives to have our own land given back to us, and for our own laws to apply on our land. I want us to have our own economy, and to have our treaties recognized. Sovereignty. Hunting and fishing rights. No taxation. I want us to be able to pursue our lives as we see fit. I want us to have what the Jews have in Israel."

"You mean for Canada and America to each have a Native country within their borders? And you expect *that* to be done?"

"Well, why not? Have you seen the size of Canada or America? Here in North America, there's more than enough land for everyone. The Vietnam war was about this same thing: the right of a people to have a democracy. The white man leaves the Native alone and vice versa. But it seems to me that the governments here just hope the Natives will fade away and disappear."

Dad, now as angry as Parry, takes a long swallow of beer and reorients himself to his immediate problem of Myles. "We're honest men, but if we're going to have our backs against the wall and need money to get Myles home, well, you and I both know a thing or two about stealing."

So says the security guard to the storekeeper. Finally Parry says, "So you really think we can rescue Myles?"

"If we put our minds to it."

Parry doesn't know what to say, and they fall silent. Even the big video screen behind the dance floor is blank. Then Parry says what Dad has known for a very long time. "Myles is the person I love most in this world. Maybe he's the *only* person I love in this world, though I wouldn't say that to anyone but you. And the funny thing is, as he grew up he wasn't afraid of many people, and the Lower East End is full of mean streets and nasty people. But he was always afraid of his mum, because he didn't understand her, and he feared people he couldn't understand." Parry thinks for a moment. "I couldn't think of any way to get Myles and his mum to make friends with each other, though Christ knows I tried. Maybe if he'd had that sort of relationship with her, things would have turned out better for him."

"Well, we have to deal with what we have in front of us right now," Dad says. "I know you love Myles, and that he loves you, too, and it doesn't mean shit what his mum thinks. Your son and my daughter are going to have a child, and the child will need his father around—hell, we'll all need Myles around, because he's one of us—and the way to do that is to quit pissing and moaning about how shitty life is and to do something about this predicament we're in. So let's do what we have to do. OK?"

Parry nods, finishes his beer and stands up straight. "I hear ya, brother. Let's give 'em hell."

...

Myles' trial still has no firm date, and Beadle is getting exasperated. So am I, but at least I have the consolation of knowing that our lawyer cares about his incarcerated client. At first I considered him indifferent, just another legal eagle out to manipulate the system to line his own pockets. He had been counsel of sorts to the Lower East End Community Center, doing a small amount of pro bono work for whatever publicity it might generate. Rose approached him when our troubles began, alternately flirting with and intimidating him to represent Myles. Beadle did so, certainly with some reluctance, only to find that the muck was thick and fragrant; instinctively, he kept raking it. He learned, quickly enough, that the Crown's case against Myles was wafer-thin and yet a conviction was entirely possible. Beadle, an ambitious but idealistic young lawyer, was surely being stigmatized somehow by the legal community for defending Myles. It didn't help that I was suspicious of him, Rose pestered him, Mum was ambivalent about him and Dad simply wrote him off as another Northup University law school alumnus out to hustle up a few bucks.

When my lover's problems first began and I found myself in that musty building where Beadle had his office, I was cynical towards him, although I am by nature not inclined towards cynicism. He and I were wary of each other, he speaking to me so carefully that his sentences were separated by epic pauses. But soon I realized that the Canadian justice system was a maddening maze, and that Myles and I were simply going to have to rely on Beadle to patiently guide us through. The lawyer himself began to view Myles's case as something remarkable and frightening, ugly, racially, culturally and politically charged and potentially controversial, had the local news media felt inclined to cover it, which they did not. He even began to view gaunt, menacing-looking, ponytailed Myles as a gentle soul who meant harm to no one.

Beadle pressed for a prompt beginning for the trial, but the courts were backed up, and empathic or at least sensible judges were rarities, too. He seemed intimidated by the Crown's office, as I imagined so many other criminal defense lawyers were. He wanted a judge to decide the case, not a jury; for what group of a dozen ordinary citizens would acquit someone like Myles, who looked like a poster boy for rage and alienation?

Beadle has also gotten in to see Peter, but Myles' old chum is so haggard and ravaged that the lawyer doubts that anyone, a judge or jury, would believe such an individual as he tries, from the witness stand, to save Myles.

Our life continues. Mum takes me down to the Army and Navy discount department store a few blocks away for the least expensive maternity clothes in Canada. I'm surely going on maternity leave soon, and am spending every possible moment with Myles.

Dad is getting as many overtime security shifts as he wants—the work is so unpleasant that lots of guys call in sick or quit—and Parry is doing what he swore he would never do: discreetly allow local drug dealers to do business in his washroom; they pay him a hefty fee for this service. Dad and Parry have a don't-ask-don't-tell arrangement with the rest of us so that if they get caught it's not our problem. Their consciences are clear as they go about their daily lives; by now, they would happily resort to terrorist tactics to get Myles out of Bayporte City Jail.

. . .

Mum, the world's most reluctant traveler, goes in with me to see Beadle to get more details on her Seattle mission.

"Mrs. Chu is in East Seattle, where there is a sizable

Chinese community. I do not envy you, because Seattle is a huge, sprawling city, and to try to confront one person who doesn't wish to be found and to try to persuade her to come back up here..."

Mum chuckles. "We've already decided that. I'm going down there alone."

Beadle shrugs. "Just so," says Beadle. "And here's this." He hands Mum a wallet-sized picture."

"I'm guessing this is Mrs. Chu," Mum says. She passes the picture to me. The woman looks pleasant enough, even pretty, but as the old racist joke goes, *They all look alike to me.* I wouldn't want to be the one going down there to find this particular Chinese woman in a crowd of Chinese women.

Mum puts the picture and computer printouts into her purse and snaps it shut. "That picture," she says.

"Where did it come from?"

"The Dragon Club," Beadle says.

"I didn't know she had a job."

"She doesn't. It's her hangout. Her boyfriend, Bobby Lee, works there. He's about Myles' age."

"So," Mum asks the lawyer, "what do you want me to do now?"

"I want you to go down there and make my job easier by bringing her back with you and save the day."

Mum smiles. "Oh, is that all?"

"By the way," he asks, "do you have a picture of Myles handy?"

"I do," I say. "It's one of us together."

"Even better. Give it to your mother so she can show it to Mrs. Chu when the time comes."

I do as told. Mum puts the picture in her purse and stands up. "Well, guy," she says, shaking Beadle's hand, "let's just hope Superwoman, when she gets down to Seattle, has one more miracle left inside her."

"I'm very pleased that you're going down there, but just remember that the Crown's office has been in contact with Myles' people and the women in that household are claiming that he's a worthless so-and-so." He pauses. "If the mother and sisters of the accused say damning things in court about Myles, this will hurt our case significantly." The lawyer sighs.

Mum sighs, too. "At least I know where we stand."

Beadle smiles at her and winks, saying with good humor, "Just make sure you don't fuck up."

I resolve to destroy Mrs. Parry and her two bitches if this whole mess we are in results in my man's destruction. But I just offer Beadle my most sincere smile and handshake. Moments later, Mum and I are in the elevator, heading back down into the lobby.

I remember moving into the loft Myles and I finally found, not far from skid row, and celebrating by conceiving our child on the building's roof that very night. Wasserman, the guy who rented it to us and whose family owned it, was a wannabe artist, swarthy and animated, with a goatee and a beret. He no more wanted to be running this property than I wanted to spend my life at the Dunsmuir perfume counter. Wasserman liked us because he could see we were in love, and he was, as they say, in love with love. I think, frankly, he also fell in love with Myles and felt jealous of me. The loft was airy and spacious, with a hardwood floor and several windows; a kind of trapdoor led to the rooftop, to which only we had access. "You can think of the rooftop as a second floor of your apartment," Wasserman said, as if the loft were already ours. "You can have dinner parties up here, or just hang out. You can even sleep out here, if it's one of Bayporte's few rainless nights."

We got the money together and I brought it over to him as fast as I could. When Myles was busted not long afterwards, Wasserman both offered to return the money and promised not to rent the loft to anyone else till we cleared up Myles' legal troubles and were ready to resume our tenancy. Wasserman said, "You were meant for that loft, and it was meant for you; that's just the way it is. Far be it from me to disrupt the harmony of the universe."

"Nice enough building," Myles said. "But what if there's a fire?"

"No fires. This is Bayporte. The rain will put them out as soon as they start up."

Myles laughed. "Good answer."

"Say, you guys got a few minutes? I'll buy you a Coke." We stood on the street corner and drank our Cokes as the tourists passed by. "I know you two are from around here and don't really need any advice from me, but I'll give you some anyway. Don't worry about the riff raff down here; it's no worse than anywhere else. But beware of the cops. As you probably already know."

We already knew, but his warning frightened us just the same. We said goodbye and headed back to Myles's puny Davis Street apartment, so caught up with the excitement of the loft that we were oblivious to everything else. By the time we were on Granville Street, Myles said he wanted to stop by the liquor store that was just around the corner so he could buy some beer. I busied myself at a market, perusing the fresh vegetables outside, knowing that Myles, who loathed shopping of any kind, would buy the beer as fast as possible and hurry back to me.

I looked through the produce, as if knowing what to look for, when a white guy started looking through the vegetables, too.

Myles has always said that I go through life with my head up my ass. Well, I often do, and it wasn't until the white guy smacked me on my ass that I realized I had trouble on my hands. At first I thought it was Myles, but he wouldn't even kiss me in public. I turned around and looked at the white guy behind me.

"You like this?" he asked, holding up a long, thick zucchini. He reached down and patted the prodigious bulge behind his fly. "I got one of my own here. Wanna come back to my place and see?"

I pretended to ignore him and gathered up some tomatoes I neither wanted nor needed. But I knew this troublemaker was just getting started and this matter wasn't going to end quickly and peacefully; Myles would be back any moment. The Grand Street pedestrian traffic was brisk; inside the market were other customers. Nobody had overheard us, or at least nobody suspected harassment, and I wanted the guy out of my face before Myles came back and saw what was going on. I saw a white cop across the street and said, "Excuse me, I have to pay for these tomatoes..."

I was aware, as I always have been, that I was Native and these other people were white and some of them might think that whatever trouble was about to happen might just be my fault.

I went inside and stood in line to pay for the tomatoes. Outside, the cop stood looking into the market. The white guy was behind me with his zucchini. He had red hair and freckles; his teeth were crooked and yellow. He said, "You don't need tomatoes when I got this." He started fondling the zucchini as if masturbating.

The guy kept stroking the long green vegetable, and now it seemed as if everyone were watching us. I just wanted to get out of there. My heart pounded and my pulse raced. I tried to gesture to the cop, but the guy grabbed my arm. I spat into his face and yelled, "Fuck off!"

At just that moment, Myles walked in.

Myles, twice the guy's size, grabbed him by a hank of his red hair and spun him around as if throwing a rag doll. With one mighty shove he sent the redhead into the street. The zucchini went flying. The cop came running up to them. I stood in front of Myles, using my body as a shield in case the cop decided to shoot first and ask questions later. The redhead lay prostrate on the ground, coughing. "He came at me," I said to the cop. "He grabbed me inside the market."

Everyone at that moment seemed to look away. Then the cop looked at us, both Myles and me, then individually. I didn't want to know what he was thinking. I stayed close to Myles. The cop said, almost smirking, "How come you didn't defend her before

Red here grabbed her? Big guy like you."

"I went around the corner to buy some beer."

"Where's your beer, then?"

"They didn't have my brand."

"Were you the one who started this fight, Injun?" the cop asked Myles.

"He's not an Injun," I blurted. "He's never been anywhere near India. He and I, we're both Natives."

The cop, not expecting such respectful, logical backtalk, eyeballed us both for several long moments. Meanwhile, Red was recovering and stood up. He spat and wiped his mouth.

"I'm guessing you live nearby, Injun," the cop

said.

"Yessir," Myles said. "Main and Cordova." There was a frightening serenity in him. He was at his most dangerous just when he really seemed to have a grip on himself. It did not surprise me at all when the cop said, "Well, Injun, this is your unlucky day. You can't just pound on a guy because he sticks a vegetable in your girl's face. I'm going to arrest you for assault."

Myles would have gone straight to Bayporte City Jail if the Sikh woman who minded the store hadn't rushed out to us and said, "No, you cannot do that. The young man here was bugging the girl, making her mad, and the other one just came to stick up for her. Try to arrest the young man and I will tell the court what I know."

The cop is named Taylor, I would later learn from

our lawyer, although Bayporte police officers wear no name tag, just an odd, oval-shaped patch with a number on it. He looks around, sizing up the situation. "Well, it looks as though the incident is over." To Myles he says, "My advice to you is to go home to the reservation and keep your hands to yourself."

Myles nods and says, "Gotcha."

The Sikh shopkeeper says to me, "Your boyfriend is a gentleman. He is too good for these streets. I have been in Canada too long. Maybe I should go back to India."

After a moment of silence, the woman goes back inside, Taylor wanders off and so does the redhead. Myles takes me by the arm and leads me up Grand Street, back towards the Lower East End. Our pace is brisk; Myles is eager to be far from the ugliness that's just ended. Finally, he says, "Nedy, don't you *ever* do that again."

"Do what again?" I was not expecting an admonition from him. I was expecting, I suppose, praise for my aplomb in handling such a difficult situation.

"What you did back there."

"Which was...?"

By now he's gritting his teeth in exasperation, having to explain simple things to obtuse Nedy. "You know, defending me. I don't need you for that. I can take care of myself."

"I wasn't trying to defend you. In fact, *you* were protecting *me*."

Myles, really riled now, kicks at a piece of a broken

beer bottle and howls, "Forget it, OK? Fuck!"

I know he's right but I don't want to say anything. He's not looking at me, so he can't see the tears streaming down my face. But then he does look at me; alarmed, he takes me into his arms and kisses me. "You know I'll always love you, right? Do you think we'll last a lifetime together?"

I nod, and he kisses me some more. "Don't say anything," he tells me. "There's nothing for you to say. Are you hungry as I am? Good. Let's go to Karma and see if they'll accept my invisible Visa card."

We walk and walk; finally, we are at Karma, where Myles says, "Gurvinder, we are famished but broke. Will you serve us now and let me pay later? Like, in a couple of days?"

"Hungry but broke!" Gurvinder says. "And I

suppose you want your food on clean dishes, too?"

Myles smiles, getting the joke. "Yes, if it isn't too much trouble."

"Plus wine and dessert?"

Myles shrugs. "Sounds good to me."

Shingara smiles at me. "For you I will do this. If he shows up alone, I will tell him, as you Canadians would say, to 'piss off.'"

Both men laugh and Gurvinder leaves. Myles squeezes my hand and murmurs, "Hey."

I squeeze back. "Hey."

"Look, I didn't mean to hurt your feelings with that stuff I said to you a little while ago. You're the best girl a guy could have, and don't think I don't know it. You were just trying to do the right thing when we were dealing with that cop and that troublemaker outside the market. If it hadn't been for you, that cop would have shot first and asked questions later." He thinks for a moment. "Seems like we live in a world of bullies and dope fiends where I always have to be nearby in case someone fucks with you."

I shake my head. "Now, you know that's not true. I don't need anyone's protection. That market has been there forever and I'd been there lots of times. That was the first time I have ever had that kind of trouble. He was just a strung-out little punk looking to hassle someone."

"A strung-out *white* punk," Myles says.

"Whatever. It's ancient history now, right?"

The restaurant is filled with tables covered with

immaculate white tablecloths and the pungent aroma of authentic Indian cuisine. Our server comes back with two bloody marys, the house drink, and I enjoy it so much that it's nearly gone after two gulps. "Our dinner special tonight is the lamb curry. For those who think Pakistan is a superior country to India, I will put strychnine in. If you disbelieve that, I will leave the strychnine out."

"Then you know our answer," Myles tells him. "India rocks, Pakistan sucks."

Shingara smiles. "Correct." He disappears.

Myles looks glum. "I made a dangerous enemy today."

"Who?"

"That white cop. Taylor. Was that his name?"

I take a deep breath. Today's adventure has not become ancient history after all. It survives, and who knows when it will be forgotten.

"Taylor is really going to fuck me over," Myles says, his voice barely audible.

"You did nothing wrong."

"I did so. I undermined his authority in front of the general public."

"No, the Indian woman who ran the market undermined his authority. She reamed him. You played it very, very cool."

"And maybe that's why the cop is going after me. That Indian woman straightens him out in front of people in public, tells him what's what, makes him blush and walk away. You can't speak to the police that way. He's got to retaliate some way, and I would be his most convenient victim."

"Well," I say, "all in all it's been a good day. We finally got our loft and soon we'll be moving in."

"Fuckin' A," Myles says, and we both laugh as Shingara brings our strychnine-free lamb curry.

When two people are deeply in love, as Myles and I were, it becomes more difficult for others to determine where one ends and the other begins. This becomes even more apparent when someone or something threatens to destroy this single organism. So, that evening, with the Myles-Nedy oneness being under attack, we became, if anything, better than ever. My father had been right: *Be true to each other and keep your sense of humor. You'll see soon enough what I mean.*

Myles and I overate, then lingered over coffee,

brandy and dessert. We talked, laughed and paid no attention to the fact that we were the only ones left in the restaurant. When the bill arrived, Myles merely scribbled his name, knowing it would remain forever unpaid. "Wanna go now?"

"Yes," I said, "yes." Because there was another kind of dessert I wanted much more: Myles, alone, with me, in our apartment. We walked home arm in arm, with nothing to say. At the building's front entrance, a police cruiser was parked, its lights flashing. As soon as we entered the building, the cruiser drove off.

We conceived our child half an hour later, under a heavy blanket on the building's rooftop. Myles did not use a condom and I said nothing about it, though I knew a pregnancy would result. He held me, entered me, loved me as never before as downtown lights shone and assorted sounds echoed through the neighborhood, the rest of Bayporte apparently oblivious to the scandalous carnal fun taking place for many nearby residents to see had they been inclined to open their drapes and look.

Afterwards, Myles sleepily pulled a blanket over us, murmured my name and fell asleep. We said nothing throughout the night, for there was nothing to say. We just both knew, at least for the time being, that we had everything we wanted and needed in life.

...

Mum, refreshed, awakes from her nap as her bus races along the I-5 freeway towards downtown Seattle in the evening. She peers out the window at the utterly unfamiliar, spectacularly lit skyline. She knows just how much she can spend on this mission, which is relatively little, and therefore must act as quickly as possible.

Minutes later, the bus parks in the Greyhound station. Mum steps down with all the others—the bus was full every moment of the trip, and their arrival coincides with that of two other, equally packed buses, whose passengers are as eager as she is to get off. She hurries across the blacktop towards the station's lobby; for the sake of convenience, she has brought along just a tote bag. Beadle has made a reservation for her at a hotel that he says is close to the Dragon, the nightclub where she will find Mrs. Chu. Inside the Greyhound lobby she sits for a moment to collect her thoughts. She thinks about having a pop from one of the vending machines but decides she doesn't have money for that. She takes a deep breath and stares out the window for several long moments.

To her, Seattle, like Bayporte, is a boomtown that stretches on forever and doesn't know when to quit, a new city where very few things are permitted to get old. The people on the bus with her, and the ones now in the lobby, are mainly, surprisingly, white; Mum had expected Greyhound riders in this huge American city to be poor blacks or browns, while white people, the moneyed visitors and the business travelers, would be flying into Sea-Tac Airport. Crossing the border, she felt like the only redskin the white U.S. Customs officer had ever seen. She had cleverly devised her explanation for going on this unlikely, crucial trip. He asked her the usual questions and believed her lies.

Everything Mum feels about America is conditioned by her awareness of American power: America as the badass police officer whose beat is Planet Earth, with six billion people very much at

America's mercy. With a good ol' boy known as Dubya in the White House (whose daddy, a former president, got him his job) and his predecessor being impeached because he lied when, under oath, he said he did *not* fuck that intern in the Oval Office. To Mum, America is still pretty much the same yahooland of those cornball Hollywood movies. The crucial difference, obviously, is that today, with Soviet communism dead and the Cold War over, what is happening in America matters more than ever.

Mum thinks she can view American power with more objectivity because she lives outside the United States. While America is rich, she can see that virtually all Americans are not. The quality of American life, with its gadgetry and secondhand cars and box architecture saturating the senses, is ludicrous, so the people hurry to psychiatrists for tranquilizers and antidepressants for relief from the inevitable anxiety. This happens in Canada, too, but it started in the States.

America is surely the world's most conservative country. More than any other nation, it stands to gain by maintaining the status quo. The world seems to praise America's "energy," which presumably has enabled this country to emerge as the greatest military and economic power in history and be home to unparalleled achievements in the arts and culture. But what is this "energy," anyway? Perhaps it is something essentially toxic and expensive, a reaction to being Number One despite myriad domestic problems that leave everyone's nerves flayed. That "energy" is violence that has been sublimated into blind and insatiable consumption, showy philanthropy, uptight and offensive moral crusades and an unmatched talent for building ugly cities and filling the mass media with overbearing, talentless performers.

Obviously, America is hardly the world's only violent, unattractive and neurotic country. But today it is boss to everyone else, most of whom will never step on American soil; only luck, perhaps, prevented Dubya from pushing the button that would have vaporized Iraq in the aftermath of September 11. Luck, too, prevents the white men who control the country from using their guns to eliminate the redskins like us who somehow managed to survive. To her, this country has an us-versus-them mentality; "they" want to take it all away from "us." Mum thinks the Americans *deserve* to have it taken away.

She marches through the lobby's front doors and out onto the sidewalk, where a glass sign of a massive running greyhound is above the doors. The sky is coal-black and studded with stars, but something in the way its dampness penetrates her skin makes Mum feel as if she is still in Bayporte. She is relieved that the Greyhound station isn't in the wrong part of town, where mangy black men might panhandle her for dope money. The taxis are lined up six deep; Mum smiles when the driver of the front one emerges. He is a young Chinese man. An excellent omen. "Can I help you?" he asks.

"Yes. I need to go here..." She hands him the address.

"Oh, sure," he says, nodding. "Hop in."

She slides into the backseat of the new-smelling taxi, and at once is filled with terror and dread, not the exhilaration she had expected, or at least hoped, to feel. *Hop in. We're ready to roll. This is the impossible journey to save Myles and must not fuck up.* Mum decides to try making friends with this young Chinese man whose perfect, unaccented English indicates a familiarity with Seattle. His name, next to his unsmiling photo on the meter, says Ted Fong. He swings out onto the street and takes one turn after another, efficiently maneuvering through hideous downtown Seattle traffic. Her goal is to visit the nightclub and find Mrs. Chu and her boyfriend while remaining anonymous in a Chinese milieu. Not an easy thing, but Mum figures that's all she can do.

She's over 40, about to become a grandmother and trying to infiltrate the Chinese section of Seattle to save her grandchild's father. But she tries not to think about such things right now.

At the hotel she tips Ted a dollar and thanks him profusely. The hotel is much like the Motel 6 chain one finds throughout America. "Would you mind waiting for a moment while I get checked in? I'll need your service some more," she tells Ted.

Ted, a short-haired young man with an inscrutable narrow face, shrugs and nods. This middle-aged Native Canadian he's just driven into Chinatown has got to be the most interesting fare he's had in some time; it may be fun to stick around and become part of her adventure, and he can tell by her hurried, worried demeanor that she represents no harm to him. Clearly she needs his help, if only for transportation, but her real and more pressing needs are none of his business. He has looked at her finger and seen her wedding ring; he knows she is a mother. He has a mother, too, and his isn't much different from her. Perhaps her problems right now, and her trip to Seattle, are because of her child or children; he is willing to make himself useful to her tonight, and says so.

Mum goes inside, registers as fast as she can and hurries up to her room. She brushes her teeth, combs her hair and, before returning to Ted, looks closely in the mirror. Does she look her age? She wants to, right now. Back in Bayporte, everyone in her world knows her age, so the subject is irrelevant. Plus, she looks every day of her age because she is a Lower East End survivor. But she is now about to enter a nightclub for the first time in many years, a nightclub in a foreign city where all the customers are likely to be Chinese, and this time she has no family or rock band to fall back on. She washes her face, pulls back her hair into a sort of bun and wraps a scarf over her head. She looks like someone middle-aged who is trying to look old. Mum knows this but can do little about it, and outside Ted is waiting for her. She locks her room, hurries through the lobby and returns to the taxi, looking, she suspects, like the befuddled visitor she is.

The Dragon, another surprise, is another glittering manifestation of Seattle's wealth. In Bayporte there are few affluent Natives; in Seattle, it appears, there are few indigent Chinese. The nightclub is in the basement of a massive luxury hotel. Mum feels a pain in her stomach; her hands tremble. She would have been happier if the nightspot had been a skid-row dump.

She says to Ted, "I'm going in for a moment."

Ted nods, tacitly agreeing to wait for her. Although Mum does not know it, the entire Seattle Police Department could come roaring up, lights blazing and sirens blaring, and Ted would not budge. This Native lady, going into the Dragon? It's better than any entertainment on television.

"Yes, ma'am," Ted says, escorting her up to the Dragon's entrance. "I'll wait in the cab."

Mum, in fact, has entered not the nightclub but the lobby of the hotel; the Dragon does not actually have its own entrance. The imposing Plexiglas doors automatically slide wide open as she steps onto thick burgundy carpeting. Desk clerks, with nothing better to do and no one important around to scrutinize them, visit discreetly with each other; the bell captain leans against his desk, his mind far away. Mum, doing her best to look as if she knows precisely where she is going, heads past them to where a fancy glass sign with an arrow points down a flight of stairs. Mum heads down into the opulent basement, her heart hammering in her ears.

"Good evening, madam," says the young man at the door. Is he Barbara Chu's boyfriend? She has no idea.

"Hello. This is the Dragon, right?"

"Yes."

Feeling the need to lie, Mum says, "I'm supposed to meet someone here but I'm afraid I'm early. Mind if I sit down?"

"Come right in." He escorts Mum into a very dark, very popular nightspot and shows her to one of the few vacant tables. "The person you're here to meet...if they arrive, should I know their name?"

"Actually, it's an employee." Taking a deep breath, Mum asks, "Are *you* Bobby Lee?"

"No. He won't be in till later. Like a drink?"

"Yes, please. White wine."

He goes and she feels more comfortable, remembering her own long-ago days in nightclubs. Tonight the band is live, and she suddenly grows nostalgic for those evenings across Canada when she literally sang for her supper. She finds herself tapping her toes to the electric beat and has to admit that these places were, and are, fun. She liked being young; she resents and regrets the necessity of growing middle-aged. Throughout my childhood, Mum smiled as she occasionally spoke of those days with her band, even their misadventures that nearly resulted in missed or compromised gigs. She and her bandmate lover simply lost interest in each other and she left; had she remained, her limited vocal talents would have made maintaining such a livelihood increasingly difficult. If I have a decent knowledge of popular music—as I believe I do—it is because Mum sang them all softly throughout my childhood as she went about her housework. Sitting here in the Dragon, listening to those songs, Mum wonders if the young people who have heard those songs all their lives know what the songs themselves are about and what inspired those Tin Pan Alley musicians to write them. And if those standard songs are not understood by these young people, do the people understand themselves?

Mum, in Seattle, is alone for the first time she can remember, and this aloneness is merely physical, as she is apart from her family every day for short periods of time and surrounded by familiar sights and sounds. But tonight she is in a foreign country, listening to a familiar song sung by an androgynous young man who clearly knows the song only as a series of syllables set to a melody. *Pretty woman!* yelps the singer, his face contorted, hips pumping, a young man who needs no pretty woman, just himself. But nobody with a relevant connection to this world—through a lover, family or God—could look and sound so hopelessly onanistic. Mum is listening to the sound of hopelessness, or nihilism, in the singer's voice, and even if it is merely the fashionable nihilism that she seems to see everywhere, it captures her empathy. Deviance, a frightening thing to witness, is also captivating; these boys onstage have mastered the art. Mum applauds them as they finish the song; she sips her drink.

After a smattering of applause from the audience, the band starts playing again. Mum looks up and sees another Chinese man's face. His clothes are slightly different but his confident young face—babyishly round, hairless, small-eyed, pug-nosed—is similar to that of the man who has just left. Mum smiles in spite of herself: *They all look alike to me.*

"Mrs. Ignas?"

Mum nods. "Please sit."

He does, and they are facing each other. The music is deafening; normal conversation will be impossible in this milieu. Mum and he must rely on lip-reading and what little each can hear of the other's voice. She hates this ludicrous situation, knowing that everything is at stake and that so many are counting on her to succeed in this mission. She must simply and passionately level with this man and hope for his cooperation.

She points at him. "Bobby Lee?"

He shrugs. "Maybe. Why?"

She sips at her wine, grateful for its coldness and smoothness. She feels grateful that the room is dark and noisy and that this man probably has no idea just how nervous she is. "I don't want to see Bobby Lee. I want to see Barbara Chu"—her heart thunders as she speaks, finally, the name of the person who has been at the center of this whole ordeal.

"Why?" repeats the man, emotionless. He doesn't flinch or growl or punch Mum in the nose, as she might have expected.

"I am the mother-in-law of the man who is accused of raping her. Myles Parry. He's in prison in Bayporte."

Mum feels as if she's in a poker game. She stares at him. He stares at her. Slowly, he shows her his cards, one at a time. His full less lips curl insolently. "A fine man your daughter married."

"He *is* a fine man," she retorts. "And so is his wife."

He sips at his beer, understanding now why she's here and what she almost certainly wants Barbara Chu to do for her. He looks past her. "Barbara can't help you. Piss off."

"Myles will rot in prison for something he didn't even goddamn do. Understand?"

"How you know that?"

"Because I know!"

Bobby Lee rolls his eyeballs. Just then the band stops playing and is replaced by a sound system that is somewhat quieter. A server appears and asks if they want anything. "Give me a Coors and her whatever she's drinking."

The server disappears and Mum says, "Did you hear what I just said?"

"You said you know he didn't do it. Well, the cops and courts seem to see things differently, don't they?"

Mum leans in towards him. "Why do you think I came down all this way?"

"To get that guy's ass out of prison, obviously."

"So he can go back to work and raise his family. They're going to have a baby soon."

"What do you want me to say? 'Congratulations'?" Bobby Lee, Mum can see, is businesslike and impatient, a prosperous young first-generation Chinese-American who probably wears a Rolex and drives a BMW to work. He doesn't just work here; he *runs* the Dragon. Why should *he* care about the fate of Myles Parry?

"Do you think I would have come all this way on behalf of someone who would commit such a crime?"

He appraises her with narrowed eyes, unsure if her question is rhetorical. "I don't know you any more than you know me. I don't know what you would do."

"Do you believe I would do such a thing?" Mum persists.

Bobby Lee sighs. "Here's what I believe: that Barbara says she was raped by a man who looked like Myles Parry. That's good enough for me, and she's trying really hard to put this whole thing behind her, and *that's* good enough for me, too." He pauses. "You're going to be a grandmother, huh? Want a boy or a girl?"

Mum shrugs. "Who knows? Who cares? So long as it's healthy and gets to grow up with its mum and dad around."

Her appeal fails to have the intended effect. "Look," he asks, "why are you bugging me? I've already told you how it is."

Mum glares at him.

"See, lady, I'm an American. I don't know a thing about Canada. I'm sure you have lawyers and shit up there. Some lawyers put Myles in jail, right? Maybe some other lawyers can get him out. Check that out. But Barbara is my cousin and I don't want to see her traumatized any more than she has been and I have a feeling that you want her to go back up to Bayporte and tell the cops she was all wrong, Myles wasn't the guy, they should let the poor bastard go free. Well, that ain't gonna happen. So you've wasted your time and mine, and I don't like having my time wasted." Mum can't tell if he's nearly crying or just incensed as he gets up to leave. She grabs his arm and pulls him back down. He offers no resistance.

Mum withdraws my picture from her wallet. "Look. This is Myles. He's about your age. I'm sure you would like him. I'm sure you could relate to him."

Bobby peers at the photo, startled by Myles' long hair, the earring dangling from his left lobe. *Am I supposed to feel friendship or brotherhood with a guy who looks like that?*

Mum takes out the picture of Myles and me. Bobby

seems reluctant to look, but does so anyway. "Have you ever committed a rape?" Mum asks.

"Excuse me?" The inscrutable face shows some emotion: indignation, offense, resentment. The eyes narrow further at having this odd woman confront him in his nightclub.

"I think you heard me."

"No," he says. "No rapist here."

"Do you think I have come all this way just to give you a hard time?"

"Probably not."

"Do I seem like an idiot to you?"

"No."

"Then take that picture with you and show it to

Barbara. Tell her that he is behind bars and that he will stay there until she helps get him out. I know she was raped, but I also know that Myles didn't do it because he would never do anything like that." She gives him the name and address of her hotel. "Call me. Please."

Bobby Lee, a natural businessman, acts at all times exclusively in his own best interest. He understands what is being asked of him—a great deal—and what he stands to gain—this Native woman's gratitude, which to him means very, very little. He gets up, says, "No thanks, no way," and walks away.

Mum stares at her glass of white wine for the longest time. She wonders: if she broke the glass and used its jagged edge to slash her wrist, would help arrive in time to save her? Or would anybody even notice? Then she sits and watches the dancers, uninhibited young men and women who scarcely know, or care, that she is among them, a fortyish woman who has just failed at the most important mission of her life. She does not know what else to do, so when the server comes by, she asks for the bill.

"Compliments of Mr. Lee, ma'am."

Two free drinks. That is what she has come down to the Dragon to get. Mum leaves a two-dollar tip on the table and wanders out the door, up the stairs and through the hotel's vast lobby. Outisde, Ted is waiting for her. He smiles, waves and holds open the door for her. "When will you need my service tomorrow?"

"Let's go for ten o'clock."

Ted nods. "I can do that."

"Good deal," Mum says as the cab heads back

towards her hotel.

...

While Mum tries to save Myles, our baby grows inside me, reminding me of its presence with vicious kicks to the ribs at odd hours. Mum is in Seattle, so Rose and Dad give me whatever comfort they can. I stay on behind the Dunsmuir perfume counter, where the management is probably embarrassed about my presence yet lacks the backbone to send me home. I wish they would; I am sick of working at that place but those paychecks, insubstantial as they are, must continue arriving. Staying on till closing time means missing the six-o'clock visit with Myles.

I tell Myles that missing a visit or two these days will mean nothing at all once he's home and we're together again and he insists that I'm right, but those missed visits clearly obsess him. When they call his name, open his cell door and escort him into the visiting area, it makes life endurable, both the visit itself and the knowledge that someone on the outside still gives a damn about them. When that caring stops, the inmate is in the gravest danger.

I'm very much on Dad's mind as he cleans up my vomit one morning. Each day I puke up a variety of delicious and nutritious foods. I'm stickier and smellier than usual, and Rose would be here to do this dirty work except that there's some sort of special event at the community center and her boss is eager to show her off to the local bigshots who will be there. This creature inside me, making me bloated and grotesque, shows no gratitude for all the attention we've paid it. Its violence and the chemical imbalances necessary for its growth have made me regurgitate many meals and bump into or knock over many items. The hours behind the perfume counter sometimes make me especially nauseous, though I haven't puked there yet. *My baby, you and I will be able to see each other soon enough*, I tell the protrusion in my middle. I want to add: *Your dad will be out by then, too.*

"So," Dad says at the breakfast table, where I've just endured my second cup of hot chocolate, "do you want a normal pregnancy?"

"Yes," I say, not knowing what would possess him to ask such an inane question.

"And do you want Myles to be a happy man when he gets out?"

"Happy, happy, happy."

"Then you better tell your boss to find another

Native girl to show off their expensive perfume," he says.

"Why?"

"Because, even though we obviously need the money, we need you and the baby even more. You know that your Dunsmuir job is a joke, anyway. They aren't paying you much more than minimum wage while they charge top dollar for everything. They just keep you up there for appearances, so the world can see that they hire Natives, too. When you show up to visit Myles and you're big as a house and it's all you can do to haul yourself around, he gets worried sick about you. If you push yourself too hard, you risk a miscarriage, and if that happens, Myles won't have anything to live for. You have to think about all these things." He glares at me. "I mean it, Nedy."

I nod.

Dad lightens up a bit. "It's a cold world out there. I guess I don't have to tell you that; you've learned about it for yourself. You have your role in life and I have mine. If I could bust Myles out of prison or carry your child to term, I would. You know that, right?"

"Yes."

Dad sighs. "I've wanted to remind you of these things for some time now. You don't like hearing me pull rank on you, of course, because I'm treating you like a child and *I* hated being talked to that way when I was your age. But, shit, in a lot of ways you still *are* a child, and God knows Myles isn't much more than a boy. No boy should be locked up the way he is...it makes me sick just to think about it. But he's in there and he'll be released when he's released. But for now, what you must do is quit your job and be there for him, physically. That is your new job, effective immediately. O.K.?"

"O.K."

The next morning I have no problem with telling Rose that I'm too ill for work, and she calls in sick for me. In fact, she effectively resigns for me, and the manager is most understanding over the phone as he makes arrangements to have my final paycheck prepared.

Relieved of one of my responsibilities, I have all the time in the world to fret over the others. The job as the perfume girl was ludicrous and boring but it kept my mind off Myles and our future.

Dad told me those nightly visits would mean a lot to Myles, and he was right. I see Beadle often, too, who has very little to tell me, but those twice-daily visits to Myles make my man beam. Myles, if anything, is in better spirits as the days roll by. Our visits don't amount to much, just smiles and murmurs, for there is very little news, but my presence here is vastly more appreciated than it was at Dunsmuir. Even the guards have a peculiar admiration for me, this pregnant woman who comes by twice a day when so many other prisoners see nobody at all.

Myles knows that I love him. He *knows* it, and this knowledge sustains him.

"Wow, you're getting huge," he says, chuckling. "Sure it's not twins?"

I just laugh. Nothing else matters. The baby is kicking more, wanting its freedom. Myles is hanging in there, wanting *his* freedom, too. I pray each night that we can pull it off.

...

Ted collects Mum and, after some more aggressive driving, takes her to some Seattle neighborhood that is, she is told, the closest thing this city has to a slum. The apartment buildings here are older, much older, with peeling paint and unmowed grass. Black children loiter; music is audible through open windows.

Ted walks with Mum, happy to be her escort but apprehensive about why they're here and what the residents are making of them. Mum, they guess, is a social worker; what else could she be? The children look at the pair curiously for a moment but then return to their fun. Mum and Ted step past a broken security gate.

"This is the right address," says Ted with some

surprise. They both step cautiously up the stairs. This building, a lowrise, has outdoor walkways and the smells are mainly of old cooking and burned food.

"Here we are," Ted says as they settle at a door. "Home, sweet home. You sure she's Chinese?" He frowns. "I thought we'd all left the ghetto decades ago."

Mum just shrugs. Ted does not want to be here any more than she does. She wouldn't be surprised if he lost his nerve and went back to the taxi. He's probably worried about that, too, and she lets him off the hook. She touches his arm very gently and says, "This is my problem. Go wait in the car. I won't be long."

Silently he walks back down the stairs and disappears. Mum stares at the door for a moment and realizes that it's already open. She knocks hard, forcing it open even wider. She calls out, "Mrs. Chu? Barbara Chu?"

A small Chinese woman, with a round face and tiny dark eyes, stands in the living room, wearing a rose-colored kimono. "Ma'am?" she says, scared. "Ma'am?"

Mum stares at her. She stares back. The TV is on; the room is filled with the imbecilic laughter of a game show.

The woman swallows repeatedly. She says, "Ma'am?"

Mum watches her till she moves a few feet closer. This woman suddenly looks older and more mature, much like the picture of her in the nightclub. Mum suddenly feels faint; she leans against the door. "Mrs. Barbara Chu…?" she asks again.

"No, ma'am. That is not my name," the woman says, slowly moving towards Mum, probably wanting to make her leave. In a moment the two women are just a few feet apart, appraising each other. Mum will not leave; Mrs. Chu lacks the nerve to order her away. What is going on inside Mrs. Chu? Mum can't tell. Fear, obviously, but also empathy, for she surely knows who Mum is and why she is here.

"Ma'am," Mrs. Chu says again, "please leave. I don't know who you want but there are many buildings around here and maybe she lives in one of those. But I have places to go and things to do. All right?" Her lips curl into the tiniest smile.

Mum shakes her head. "You're the one. I have a picture of you."

Mrs. Chu feels her courage growing. "So what?

I've had my picture taken many times."

Mum takes out the picture and shows it to her. While Mrs. Chu is perusing the photo, Mum walks inside, to the center of the living room.

"Ma'am, I'm on my way out. Go now." She points at the picture. "This isn't me. It's someone else."

"You can stop calling me ma'am. My name is June Ignas."

"Well, I am not Mrs. Chu. We've never met. Why did you come here?"

"You're right. We've never met. But I know of you."

The woman frowns. "I don't understand."

"I saw Bobby Lee last night at the Dragon."

The woman nods. "I go there sometimes." With another tiny smile she adds, "Did he give you my picture? Was he bragging about me?"

Mum doesn't think it's so funny. "I got it from a Canadian lawyer who is representing Myles Parry. You said he raped you."

Mrs. Chu pushes the photo back into Mum's hands and looks away.

"Is he the one? Is he?"

"You don't know a thing about it," Mrs. Chu says, her face full of contempt. She walks over and sits on her sofa. "You don't know what it's like. If you did, you wouldn't be here, asking me these things."

Mum, uninvited, walks over and joins her on the sofa. Their legs are practically touching.

The TV is still on. Mum has noticed, many times, how even the poor or almost-poor—perhaps that includes us—own TVs. They own radios and other gadgets, and at this moment probably half the music players in the neighborhood are blaring away through open windows. This cacophony of sound grates on Mum's nerves, and she wonders: How does it affect Barbara Chu? Does the music continue into the night while this woman tries to sleep? If so, would her neighbors care?

Mum, not knowing what else to do, simply listens to the brash music, watching Mrs. Chu, inches away, stare catatonically ahead, as if doing so will compel Mum to leave; perhaps saying and doing nothing has worked in previous predicaments. This young Chinese woman shows no sign of cooperating; the two of them could sit silently all day long. Mum finds the grinding, pounding music increasingly intolerable. She feels the adrenalin starting to squirt into her neck, her head. Maybe this is the start of a panic attack—she hasn't had one of those in years. Or maybe she is simply going crazy.

Mum cannot sit still any longer. She gets up, crosses the living room and stares out the window. Children play, music blares, untended patches of grass grow. Somewhere beyond, the rest of the city vibrates; still farther, much farther, the Lower East End grinds through another day. It occurs to her that this home she's standing in is very similar to the one she's lived in for so many years. Mum wants to burst into tears but doesn't dare.

"Have you," she asks, "been here all your life?"

"Why do you want to know?" Mrs. Chu asks,

agitated. "Why did you come here? Do you want me to go back up to Bayporte with you and say he didn't rape me? I won't do that. I have friends here. Bobby and others." She juts out her chin in defiance.

"It's a free country," Mum says. "You can do whatever you want. I'm just trying to get my son-in-law out of jail. He didn't do anything to you or anyone else."

Mrs. Chu crosses her legs, unimpressed.

"He didn't do anything, to you or anyone else," Mum repeats.

"You're wasting your time," says Mrs. Chu. "A crime happened and someone got busted."

Mum tries a different tack. "How long did you live in Bayporte?"

"I don't remember. I should've left sooner."

Mum, to show she's in no hurry to leave, takes off her jacket and sits back on the sofa. "You're about my kids' age. I'll be a grandmother soon. I'm too young for that shit."

Mrs. Chu smiles in spite of herself. Mum asks, to throw the woman off guard, "Why did you come back here to Seattle?"

She has no answer. Finally, she says, "I have children, too. Somewhere. I don't have custody."

Mum gets up and walks over to the window. Together they gaze out at the nothingness. Mum tries to relate to this woman as an equal of sorts. "Girlfriend," she says quietly, "a lot of bad shit happens to people in this world. That's one of the few things you can count on. I have been walking this planet a lot longer than you have, and I can tell you one true thing: you can hurt a lot of people when you lie." She grabs Mrs. Chu by the shoulders. "An innocent man, soon to be a father though he's not much more than a boy, is in jail because of *you,* girlfriend, and he's going to stay there till he rots."

"I saw him. He did it."

"No. All you saw was him in a police lineup. He didn't do it. He wouldn't do it."

"How do you know?"

"Because I know him."

The woman snorts. "How well do you know him? All you know is the side of him that he chooses to show you, all sweetness and sincerity. If he's nice and polite to you, you think he's a gentleman who would never do anything wrong. But the worst murderers on Death Row can be charming when it suits them. And the man who did that awful thing to me—maybe it *was* your beloved Myles!"

"Maybe," repeats Mum softly. "Maybe. So you're not totally sure?"

Mrs. Chu shrugs. "Close enough. I was raped, there was a lineup, I picked him out, he's in prison. Justice was served."

"The rape happened in the dark. You saw a Native man, a dark-skinned man, in the dark. Right?"

"I saw a man rape me. That's what I saw."

Mum shakes the woman. "Jesus Christ, girlfriend, you're all I've got to go on! Help me."

The woman screams, a hellish shrill cry. She grabs

at Mum's arms, throws them off and rushes to the front door. "Get away! Fuck off!" she shrieks.

Mum hears voices, doors opening, footsteps outside. The taxi's unmistakable horn honks; Barbara Chu starts ranting in some foreign language to a middle-aged woman who has suddenly appeared, then falls into the woman's arms and allows herself to be led away. Mum goes outside, finds the neighbors clustered along the walkway; Ted's honking becomes more insistent.

The people stare at Mum, who is careful not to stare back. She maneuvers herself through the crowd, afraid that as she descends the stairs someone will push her. But no. she makes it to the bottom and, her jacket in one hand and the picture of Myles in the other, she half-runs towards Ted, who is leaning on the horn with the motor running. She is not entirely inside the car when he speeds off with a horrible rubbery squeal.

...

That evening, hours later, she returns to the Dragon to speak to Bobby Lee. But the man at the door insists that Bobby Lee is unavailable tonight and there is no room for her to sit.

...

The human mind is a curious thing. It goes where it will and records what it wants: sights, sounds, sensations, smells. Data we wish we could forget is imprinted forever on our consciousness. In my case, Constable Taylor became every man I saw on the street after that ugly business with the guy and his zucchini on Granville Street.

Taylor had been working the Lower East End and other parts of downtown for quite some time, so I had surely seen him many times; Rose had certainly passed by him on her way to the community center. To me he was just another ultra-white cop with the swagger and attitude they all had. Then he became more real to me: the brown hair, pasty complexion, less eyes. He had thick forearms, freckled and hairy, and a neat trim build. His voice was toneless. His less eyes scared me; they opened into a void; deep inside he was a robot, a sociopath programmed to attack all who defied him. Sometimes I saw Taylor when I was with Myles; other times I was alone. He and I didn't speak to one another, for we had nothing to say. I saw his blank face on every white man; when the phone rang late at night with a wrong number, I imagined Taylor on the line, smirking and silent. When he saw Myles and me together, he shot Myles the most vicious of looks, as if fighting to restrain himself from slamming his nightstick into Myles' scrotum. When the confrontation happened that day on Granville Street, Taylor's look said *I'm going to kill you, Injun,* and Myles' look said *No way. I won't be here that long.*

What alarmed me was that Taylor felt challenged by Myles, and if there had been violence, Myles might have been killed and Taylor wouldn't even have been punished. Though there was a police officer on the scene, no law and order existed.

Taylor and I actually had a conversation once. I was on my way to Bayporte City Jail with an armload of things I had just bought at the drugstore when I saw him coming towards me. I had thrown away the receipt and couldn't prove I had paid for the things in the bag, but that was irrelevant. I knew he wasn't interested in my shopping, and I despised him so much by then that I dread ever having anything to do with him. So I walked, and so did he, and within moments we were face to face. This was on Waverly Street; as always, there was plenty of pedestrian traffic, and plenty of vehicular traffic; the drivers were always afraid of hitting doped-up pedestrians who sprang out into traffic to escape unseen but deeply felt demons.

"Can I carry your bag?" Taylor asked.

"No, thanks. I can manage," I said, feeling spasms of fear in my empty bladder and bowels.

He wouldn't move, and I couldn't, so we stood there. He stood looking at me, so I looked back, in defiance of what I had always believed—never look into a white man's eyes, and never look into a cop's eyes. I looked into the voids of his eyes and felt humiliated, degraded, raped. I wanted to attack him, to tear his throat out so that he would draw his gun and shoot me dead, and we both would be through with this whole ugly business of living.

"I know where you live," he said. "You have a few more blocks to go. That bag looks close to bursting. It would be a shame for you to spill all your things on this filthy street."

I know where you live. He was The Man, he had a gun. He knew me—my name, address, phone number. He looked at me for the longest time, and I can imagine what ran through his mind.

"I'm here to serve and protect," he said. "Tell your Injun boyfriend I'm a good guy as long as he knows his place and doesn't get an attitude with me."

I nodded. "I'll make sure he knows. I can go the rest of the way home without any help."

He nodded, too. "Just make sure he knows. Take good care, Nedy."

I shivered, hearing him say my name. "'Bye." I went home as fast as I could and resolved never to tell Myles about my encounter with Taylor. When they came to arrest Myles, Peter was there, a little high and very emotional, crying about how the other inmates had force their erections up his ass and down his throat. He repeated that he wouldn't have wished any of that upon his worst enemy. Myles rocked the big man in his arms as I put on some tea for the three of us. And that's when the cops came by to collect Myles.

...

Myles is doing what he does best and loves most. A

piece of wood sits before him, shapeless, and he ponders its future. The area around him is strewn with half-finished projects. I can see him but I'm not there.

His smiles at his tools, and I'm not sure if he's simply admiring them or if he wishes to coax their cooperation, for the work ahead is theirs as much as his. Myles doesn't want to touch the wood, much as a writer shies away from the blank page. He scrutinizes the raw chunk of wood, as if seeking an area marked PLEASE START HERE. Finding none, he wipes away tears of uncertainty about his work and himself. That uncertainty both paralyzes and mobilizes him. Without it, he cannot live.

He fondles a chisel, uses it to make the lightest of nicks on the wood, puts down the tool and opens a beer. He stares at the tool, then at the wood.

"Fuck you," he tells the latter.

He puts down the beer, picks up the chisel and approaches the wood. After several minutes of apparently aimless staring, he begins rubbing, slicing, scraping. The artist is at work.

Myles' eyes fly open in the darkness. The dream ends. He is alone in his temporary cell, which is much too small for a man his size. There is a toilet just inches away, and it reeks almost as much as he does.

He looks straight ahead and asks himself what time it is, but such a question is irrelevant. He sees his worn-out shoes on the floor and longs to put them on and sprint out of here. He remembers, again, why he is here, of the crime he has been accused of committing, a crime he cannot imagine.

He reminds himself that he must stay sane, but wonders if he is going crazy, or if he already has; is there some point he has crossed without knowing it? Maybe, he thinks, he has not gone mad, but simply died and gone to Hell. He thinks back to the First Nations Church, which he has not visited in years, and what the preacher said about Hell, the usual Christian admonitions about demons and fire. *You're wrong*, he wants to say, *it's much worse than that.*

He is alone, for now, and afraid. He dreads the time when the guard will take him downstairs, to join the general prison population. On the outside, on the streets, he is a man's man, unafraid of others; he knows who and what he is.

But these other inmates trouble him deeply. He is convinced that they perceive him as fresh meat, paralyzed with fear; his virgin ass remains unsodomized for now. He knows that a chubby white lawyer, Beadle, is in a musty office down the block, the only man fighting for Myles' freedom. Will he remain in prison forever?

The corridor beyond his cell is dimly, artificially lit. Myles stinks and itches intolerably; when had they last let him shower? Have the authorities forgotten him altogether? He tries to remember everything he has read about prison—the nighttime shivs, the gang control of entire tiers, the blow jobs given openly—and shudders. Better just try to forget.

He pictures Parry at the smoke shop, doing business as usual. He imagines me and what I might be doing just then. Myles has always found it impossible to picture a world he doesn't inhabit; how can we possibly survive without him? And how can he possibly survive without us?

Since his incarceration, he has taken up cigarettes again. He lights a Player's and inhales deeply. His penis springs erect, despite his wishes. Instinctively, he masturbates, his touch deft and experienced. He stops for a moment, drags on his cigarette and commands himself to stop. But it is no use; his hand stays busy. He wriggles out of his clothes and soon is nude underneath the single, insubstantial blanket, his hand pumping furiously. He arches his back, rejects the many fantasies that fight for his attention and shrieks silently, his face contorted. Aggh. His hand pumps and pounds, his penis stiff and sweaty, the tears streaming down his face. Awww. He gives himself over to pleasure, no longer smelling the putrid air streaming into his nostrils, for the moment forgetting this entire nightmare that his life has become. Ohhh. He is past the point of no return. Presently he ejaculates, his penis, like a fountain, squirting milky semen that lands all over his groin and stomach. By the time he has cleaned himself up, or tried to do so, he has returned, mentally, to the desolation that is his life and faded into a brief, restlessness nap.

The guard shakes him awake and escorts him down to see me in the visitors' room. He looks better than I would have guessed, which is really no compliment at all.

"Hi, sweetie," he says into the phone, as if he's just awakened, which of course is the case.

"Keep that smile on your face," I say. "It becomes you."

"Tell me something to keep this smile on my face," he says, as if issuing a challenge. I expect him to frown at any moment, just to annoy me.

"Beadle is working like hell to get you out of here."

"Gee, that's wonderful. Give him a kiss for me." He's starting to fade already. Sarcasm was never Myles's thing.

"Beadle says he can get your court date confirmed fairly soon," I tell him.

"Like when?"

"Like soon."

"Christmas is soon," he says. "Will that be my gift?"

"Your gift," I say, patting my stomach, "is right here."

"And how *is* my gift?" he asks, brightening a little.

"Even meaner than its daddy. Kicking me all the time."

He chuckles. "Sounds like my kid. Maybe call him Myles, Junior." Then, "How is Parry?"

"Spending most of his time at the smoke shop. Trying not to think about...stuff." I shrug.

"I haven't seen him lately. When's he coming by?"

"Tomorrow, with the lawyer."

"How is the rest of my family?" he asks.

"I assume everything's about the same. I don't speak to them much. It's awkward."

He nods. "I know. Your mum back from the States soon?"

"Tomorrow or the next day."

Myles rolls his eyeballs. "She went down to get that woman to come back up here and clear me of all charges. Mission impossible, eh?"

"Mum can be pretty persuasive, you know."

"Nobody's *that* persuasive."

The baby kicks. I wince. "The baby gets angry with its father's pessimism." Then, "Mum says that Beadle could really tear Mrs. Chu apart on the witness stand, really make her look like a fool. Mrs. Chu has a psychiatric history and a checkered past, so he'd bring that up so the jury would think she was nuts."

"And maybe she hates Natives, too. Those Chinatown shopkeepers have been complaining, you know, about being only a block from the Lower East End, where all us redskin weirdos are walking around on dope, going into Chinatown and panhandling the tourists."

I laugh. "Actually, my sister says most of our weirdos are at the community center all day, eating cheap meals and watching TV."

"Well, anyway, I'm not keeping my fingers crossed that your mum is going to come back holding hands with Mrs. Chu. What about that cop, Taylor?"

"I think Beadle said Taylor's already accidentally killed one Native, so Beadle may sort of play the race card, like they did in the O.J. Simpson case."

"Tell Beadle not to tell anyone that Constable

Taylor killed a Native. The jury would probably think Taylor had done the city a favor."

I shake my head. "Sweetie, you need to stay positive. We shouldn't get an attitude and talk that kind of crap."

Myles nodded. "I hear ya. Are you as tired of all this bullshit as I am?"

"You have no idea. It's just that we have to keep our shit together. We can't let our anger get out of control."

"Yeah. I try to remind myself of that, but sometimes it just doesn't work. Sometimes because I'm always here, I start to see things and hear voices and start to wonder if I'm losing my mind. If that happens, I might as well just stay here because I won't do you and the baby any good if I ever get out.

You know, I thought I was such a badass, always throwing my weight around and bossing everyone like King Shit, but now I know I'm just a kid. A kid who doesn't belong here because I haven't done anything that bad." He sighs and looks straight at me. "Nedy—do you believe me?"

I smile at him. "I believe you...and I believe *in* you, just like I believe in that ponytail on your head that's growing all the way down to your ass."

He grins, smoothing out his unruly, oily hair. "It itches like hell, too."

"You need a shampoo and a shower. I can smell you right through the Plexiglas."

Just then The Man appears, the one who wants to take my man away from me. Myles sees him, too, and slowly rises to leave. With nothing else to say to each other, we extend our arms and clench our fists, smile at each other and go our separate ways. We both feel more optimistic than we have in a long time, but of course there is no reason for us to see things in such a positive light.

...

Mum walks home from the Bayporte bus station, swearing never to take Greyhound again, and tells us her story. Our positive light begins to dim. "I hung around Seattle a day or two after Barbara Chu started bawling. I thought, 'There must be *some* way I can get her to come up here and help us help Myles.' But no, it looked pretty hopeless. Ted, the taxi driver, said he was afraid to go back into that neighborhood. So was I. Mrs. Chu wasn't about to cooperate with me, anyway. We're just going to have to deal with the charges Myles is facing and hope our lawyer can get him off." She sips at her Blush Chablis and, after a pause, says, "But her return to Seattle hurts the Crown's case, too."

"That it does," Dad says, with a loud breath that expresses everyone's exasperation with the whole matter.

Mum drains her drink and says, "Well, I'm tired. Time for bed."

Dad says, "Me, too." Together they saunter into the bedroom. Rose and I so often feel we are the adults now; I'm surprised Mum and Dad didn't ask us for permission to go to bed. The baby kicks me in the ribs, telling me it is *our* bedtime, too.

. . .

Mum's visit to Seattle, on the face of it, was

unsuccessful; Parry has been waiting, both eagerly and anxiously, for a report. Dad feels compelled to be the one to tell him, though he waits till the smoke shop closes for the day. Parry, hearing the news at work, would be distraught, unable to function. So Dad waits for the shop to close and takes Parry around the corner to Drysdale's Pub for a beer. Afterwards, Parry can go home and tell his wife and daughters about what he has just learned, if his women are still inclined to learn of Myles's fate.

"So," says Parry, "Myles will stay locked up until this Chu woman decides to do the right thing by coming up here and saying, 'Gee, maybe it wasn't him after all.'"

Dad nods. Parry is calm and soft-voiced, like his son when Myles is reaching the breaking point. "Or maybe we can get Myles out on bail."

"When? How much?"

"Don't know. Maybe it'll be set tomorrow or soon after."

"And maybe they'll say, 'Fuck it, there is no bail.'"

"Well, that's the wrong attitude," Dad says, sensing the rage smoldering inside Parry. He continues sitting there, sipping his beer, hoping Parry will not end up throwing a temper tantrum right inside the pub.

"She's down in Seattle and we're up here. And Myles is in the can," Parry says. "It's absolutely fucked."

"No. There's still hope," Dad reminds him. "Stay optimistic. Maybe all this shit will work itself out."

Parry rolls his eyeballs. "And maybe my old lady will pray tonight for Myles' release and the Almighty will get off His ass and make it come true. Amen."

Dad waves this off. "What we have to do, I guess, is just get him out. It wasn't us who put Myles in jail. It wasn't even that Chink bitch, when you think about it. It was the cops and courts who don't give a shit if an innocent man goes to jail just as long as someone gets punished after a crime is committed." Dad's voice is shaking; his teeth are clenched. Drysdale's is quiet; or at least Dad and Parry can't hear anything except each other.

"I guess my son was just born into the wrong family," Parry says, shaking his head. "His mother and her religious crap that's come to a consequence of absolutely nothing. His sisters, if you ask me, should have been working the streets to raise money for their brother's defense instead of putting out for every asshole at Bayporte City College."

Dad pictures the Parry women and comes to realize, or at least to believe, that the daughters *do* love their father and brother, although they seldom know how to show their feelings or have the courage to try. They know as well as everyone else how difficult this ordeal has been and would happily assuage him if they could. But they cannot do much for him, and perhaps Parry cannot forgive them for their inability to help, any more than he can forgive his own futility.

Dad and Parry both stare at the pub tabletop, unable for the moment to look at each other. It flashes through Dad's mind how clean the air is in here; the smokers, due to a citywide law passed several years earlier, are confined to their own room at the back. Dad wonders how Parry can afford to stay in business when so many people are cutting back on their seven-dollar packs of cigarettes, Parry's main source of income.

Parry remains silent as tears begin streaming down his face. Dad watches for a few minutes, sees that Parry isn't close to collecting himself and says, "Nevermind all that blubbering, guy. You need to hold it together. We have big things to do. Are you going to be up to it?"

Parry, with some difficulty, stops crying and wipes his eyes with his sleeve. "Yeah, I'll be up to it."

"Go home and have dinner. Get some sleep. We can get busy tomorrow. Understand?"

Parry nods, his chin thrust out. "Yeah, I understand."

When I explain to Myles that the trial has been postponed, and that Mrs. Chu's adamant refusal to return to Bayporte complicates matters considerably, he merely shrugs. "What else is new? I didn't think your mum had much of a chance anyway, going down there to see Chu."

I see Myles' eyes better than I have in a long time. He has lost so much weight that his features appear more prominent in his narrowed face. He also seems more comfortable here now, or perhaps just less uncomfortable. Within him, I think, there is an absolute lack of faith in the Canadian justice system and the growing suspicion that he may be in here for a long time. If so, he is teaching himself survival. He is goddamned if he will let incarceration destroy him.

"*You* hangin' in there?"

"Shit, sweetie," I say, blushing, "I'm not the one who has to sleep in here. The baby and I are quite comfy, thanks for asking."

"No problem." He nods as he has always done, nodding with deep understanding at the answer to a pointless question asked out of courtesy, or asked because he could not think of anything else to ask.

"You're wasting away to nothing," I tell him.

He pats his belly. "Oh, I've lost a few pounds, but I needed to lose it anyway. But when I get out, I'll put it back on and then some." He points at my very pregnant figure. "I'll start looking like you." He smiles. A big, warm smile, and for a fleeting moment

I am convinced that everything, ultimately, will be OK.

Love.

Time is up. He stands, I stand. We give our Black Power salute, then go our separate ways.

. . .

Myles understands why he is in jail, even if he doesn't accept the reason for it. But the comprehension is there, and this enables him to observe the other inmates with a previously absent empathy. Everywhere, he sees other men not much older than himself, a few even slightly younger, none of them appreciably dumber or smarter than himself. So, while the others have not been accused of raping Chinese women who could pass by them unrecognized on the street, they have committed infractions, of course. But does that warrant imprisonment? There are men in here who have stolen because they felt they had no other options and were not shrewd enough, or lucky enough, to avoid capture. Most of these men are in here for nonviolent crimes; but to the people running the establishment, Myles thinks, theft is as bad as murder. *Steal food when you're hungry and they'll put your ass in jail. Is that how it works?*

I bring him cigarettes from the smoke shop and pornographic magazines that the other men enjoy as much as Myles does. They are all in here together; distancing oneself from the others is not an option. He knows that even the most personable of these men may be the most vicious, but there is little he can do about it. Indeed, he returns to solitary confinement after getting into a brutal fight with a white man who tries to sodomize him. Myles sports a black eye from the altercation but brags to me of the number he did on the other guy. The experience matures him, or perhaps merely steels him; he has won the first round of what may become a very long and difficult fight. The next bouts may be against more fierce opponents but he has established a reputation as someone who can hold his own. He sits through our visits with fewer complaints about his living conditions; he is determined to see his baby smile when it arrives, and maybe even hold it in his arms some day.

The good news, as Beadle delivers it, is actually bad: the bail has been agreed to, but it is high, much too high for us to raise. And the summer rolls around, its appearance marked by a week of glorious sunshine which reminds us, as if we need a reminder, that time will not be patient with us.

...

To cheer myself up, I went to Nirvana for dinner. Gurvinder drove me home that evening, and I'd become quite a behemoth by then. Even breathing wore me out, and I prayed to the little bugger inside me to hurry up and get out.

I needed cheering up because I had not seen Myles in the longest time. He had gotten into that fight with the guy who tried to rape him, and once in solitary he screamed and acted out, so they kept him isolated until he calmed down. I had waddled into the visiting center and seen him. He looked emaciated, bony, disoriented; on other visits he looked more than capable of tolerating prison life. He proved himself impossible to size up; when he smiled, I saw the real Myles, alive and presumably well.

"You're starting to look like those addicts on Waverly Street. Wasting away to nothing," I told him.

"Tell my mum to have her buddy Jesus get off his ass and rescue me," he replied.

"We're working on the bail money," I said.

"That's nice."

We had nothing to say, so we just sat and gazed at each other. That was enough. It was a highly erotic experience. Many people, naked and in bed, don't have such good sex as our zipless fuck through that wall of Plexiglas.

"You know," he said finally, "if I get out of here,

it's because I've decided I can survive in here. That's one of the weird things about life: once you've lost everything, you can have it all. Once you stop thinking, you really start learning." He paused. "Maybe I'll never get out of here. But if that happens, I won't stop growing."

"Whatever happens," I told him, "I'll be here, by your side. I won't stop growing, either."

"And if I do get out, I'll build us the best furniture anyone's ever seen. I'll build us a dinner table that will last forever. You know that baby inside you? His *grandchildren* will be eating at that table."

I smiled at my man's little fantasy. The baby, sensing where we were and why, kicked with rage. I stared past Myles, at the two guards standing by the entrance. The baby said, *Let them who are without sin cast the first stone.*

I snapped out of my reverie and found myself alone, in our living room. The baby's kicks were real. My time was approaching. The phone rang and with some effort I made it across the room and answered. It was Talia. "Have you seen my dad lately?" she asked, her voice shaking.

"No. Isn't he usually at the smoke shop?"

She burst into tears.

"Talia!" I practically screamed. "What's happening. Tell me!"

"The smoke shop is closed! You know Dad was making money for Myles' bail by letting the pushers sell in the back room, right? Yesterday one of the buyers was an undercover cop. Dad was on his day off so he didn't get busted, but he's disappeared and the cops want him."

We were both silent for a moment. The baby kicked furiously but for the first time I didn't mind. In fact, I barely noticed. "Nedy—?"

"I'm right here, Talia. I don't know what to say. I don't know where he could have gone."

"You wouldn't tell my anyway. You don't like me."

"Talia, I hardly know you. We've had some words, but that's all. You've always done your thing and I've done mine. Our families aren't close. We just have Myles in common. And you *know* I love Myles, so I have to love the rest of you crazy people, too."

She chuckled in spite of herself. "If Dad calls?"

"If he calls, you'll be the first to know."

"Thanks." She hung up. I did, too, and just then Mum unlocked the front door and walked in. "Nedy," she asked, "why do you look so upset?"

"Talia just called. Parry's Smoke Shop was busted late last night because of an undercover drug deal. Parry was on his day off. He's gone missing." Mum's face looked as I imagined it might have down in Seattle, trying to talk Barbara Chu into coming up here to help save Myles. "Has Dad seen him?" I asked.

Mum shook her head. "Parry hasn't been by here. If he had come by, I would have known about it." She came over to me and said, "Well, Parry's been all out of sorts since Myles was arrested. Whatever happens, it's not our problem. How do you feel? All right?"

I shrugged. "Tired. Old. Fat."

She smiled. "Me, too. Want a Tia Maria?"

"Yes, please."

She disappeared and returned presently with the liqueur.

"They tried to rape Myles in there, you know, but he fought back, so they threw him into solitary." I shook my head.

"Better not to think about such things," Mum said. "They couldn't destroy him if they tried. He's got too many of us on the outside who love him, keeping him strong."

I sipped the coffee liqueur and sat back, waiting.

For what, I couldn't say; but it seemed there was nothing left for me to do but wait: For the baby, for its father, for its grandfather. I hated waiting, whether it was waiting on the rich bitches at Dunsmuir or sitting there on my ass in my living room. Waiting can be as difficult as anything you'll ever do.

"Rose says we're getting closer to the bail amount, so let's just stay cool and keep our fingers crossed," Mum said.

Just then we heard the door being opened down the hall and Mum rushed towards it. Dad had come home. He and Mum spoke in quiet voices as I strained to listen. Soon the two walked into the living room, both of them ashen-faced.

Parry, Dad informed me, had been found dead in

the back room of the smoke shop. "He shot himself with that gun he kept under the counter that no one was ever supposed to know about. The smoke shop has been closed by the police."

"Has anyone told Myles yet?" I asked.

"No."

"Then it's best if I tell him," I said.

"You'll have to wait till visiting hours tomorrow. It's too late now."

Mum looked at me queerly. "Are you all right, Nedy?"

I took a deep breath and couldn't think of anything to tell her that might make sense. I felt the wisdom of the ages swirl about the room and I felt a connection I'd never before experienced between my mother and myself because I knew that I, too, was about to become a mother. For a moment all that existed for me was her, and then a moment later all I could see and think of was Myles. I threw back my head and let out a hellish scream. My waiting was over.

...

Myles is chiseling the wood, nearly fighting with it but enjoying this battle all the same. From a distance, his child cries, the inconvenient hour irrelevant, the wailing demanding but not miserable, into the still night air the cries go on and on and on, loud and shrill enough to shatter glass and wake the graveyards.

ABOUT THE AUTHOR

George Onstot was born in San Francisco but has lived in
Nevada, Washington, Nebraska and Ontario. For the past
many years he has been living in Vancouver,
where he is at work on his next novel.